"The marriage must b

Gage laughed. "Do you really think that's possible, Fallon, after the way you were crawling all over me last night?"

"I—I..." Fallon started, but then stopped. It appeared as if she was regrouping. "I don't want to muddy the waters and complicate what is essentially a business arrangement. You must see that."

"No, I don't." Gage plopped his beer on the nearby cocktail table, causing some to spill over. "What I see is a woman afraid of taking what she wants. You and I know that this isn't just about business, Fallon. It never was."

Her eyes narrowed. "What is it?"

"It's a reckoning. Between you and me. About what we both wanted but didn't happen that night. Don't you think it's time we find it?"

* * *

His Marriage Demand is the second book in The Stewart Heirs series from Yahrah St. John.

Dear Reader,

His Marriage Demand is the second book in The Stewart Heirs series. My inspiration for the series was the '80s soap opera *Dynasty*. I loved the name Fallon and used it for my heroine.

Fallon Stewart is in need of a bailout for her family's company, Stewart Technologies. The former housekeeper's son, Gage Campbell, has become a wealthy financier despite Fallon's past lies, which caused his mother to lose her job with the Stewarts. Gage demands marriage in exchange for his help, but he has a secret agenda. I love that both Fallon and Gage are flawed. Hope you cheer them on, as I did, as they let go of the past to find happiness.

For information on Dane Stewart's story—the final book in the trilogy—or to find my backlist titles, visit my website and sign up for my newsletter at www.yahrahstjohn.com, or write me at yahrah@yahrahstjohn.com.

Best wishes,

Yahrah St. John

YAHRAH ST. JOHN

———

HIS MARRIAGE DEMAND

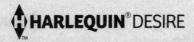

Recycling programs
for this product may
not exist in your area.

ISBN-13: 978-1-335-60383-8

His Marriage Demand

Copyright © 2019 by Yahrah Yisrael

This edition published by arrangement with Harlequin Books S.A.

For questions and comments about the quality of this book, please contact us at CustomerService@Harlequin.com.

® and TM are trademarks of Harlequin Enterprises Limited or its corporate affiliates. Trademarks indicated with ® are registered in the United States Patent and Trademark Office, the Canadian Intellectual Property Office and in other countries.

Printed in U.S.A.

Yahrah St. John is the author of thirty books. When she's not at home crafting one of her spicy romances featuring compelling heroes and feisty heroines with a dash of family drama, she is gourmet cooking or traveling the globe seeking out her next adventure. St. John is a member of Romance Writers of America. Visit www.yahrahstjohn.com for more info.

Books by Yahrah St. John

Harlequin Desire

The Stewart Heirs

At the CEO's Pleasure
His Marriage Demand

Harlequin Kimani Romance

Cappuccino Kisses
Taming Her Tycoon
Miami After Hours
Taming Her Billionaire
His San Diego Sweetheart

Visit the Author Profile page at Harlequin.com for more titles.

You can find Yahrah St. John on Facebook, along with other Harlequin Desire authors, at www.Facebook.com/harlequindesireauthors!

To my best friend and sister,
Dimitra Astwood, who passed away
while I wrote this, but will live on in my heart.

Prologue

Fallon's hands trembled with anger as she placed the phone receiver in its cradle. Rising from her chair, she strode across her stylishly appointed corner office and stared out the window overlooking downtown Austin. Although she understood why her older brother, Ayden, wasn't returning her calls, she was still annoyed he'd gone to Jamaica while she was in such a desperate state.

Stewart Technologies was on the brink of bankruptcy. As CEO, Fallon had done her best to keep the company afloat, working sixty- and eighty-hour work weeks, but she was bailing water from a sinking ship. The last few weeks she'd been unsuccessful in her attempts to secure a bank loan.

She'd gone to Ayden, the black sheep in the Stewart family, for assistance nearly a month ago. Ayden had

rejected her assertion that he help the "family business." The more Fallon thought about it, why should
Ayden rescue the company started by a father who
would never claim him as his son? Ayden owed no al-
legiance to her or any other Stewart for that matter.

Was it any wonder he'd ignored her calls?

Although she'd acquired personal wealth of her own
through sound investments, Fallon wasn't in a position
to bail out the company. Her baby brother, Dane, certainly wasn't about to, either. He, like Ayden, wanted
nothing to do with Stewart Technologies. Dane was
happiest in front of a camera being someone else, and
it served him well. He was an A-list actor and got paid
millions of dollars. Fallon doubted he'd put up his hard-
won earnings to save a company he'd never wanted any
part of in the first place.

What was she going to do?

"Perhaps you should let it fail," Shana said when
they met up for drinks at their favorite martini bar
across town an hour later. Shana Wilson was one of
Fallon's favorite cousins on her mother's side. Nora
hated them spending time together because she tried
to disassociate herself from her back-country roots.
But Fallon didn't care. Shana was loud and opinionated but down-to-earth.

Fallon stared at Shana incredulously. After all the
hard work she'd put into Stewart Technologies, intern-
ing in the summer while home from Texas A&M University, learning the business from the ground up and
climbing the ladder to finally sit in the CEO chair,

she was supposed to give it all up? "Have you lost your mind?"

Shana chuckled. "Don't have a coronary. It was just a suggestion. I hate seeing you stressed out."

An audible sigh escaped Fallon's lips. "I'm sorry, Shana. I know I haven't been a joy to hang with lately."

Shana had come dressed for the evening. She was wearing a glittery sleeveless top, miniskirt, strappy heels and large gold-hoop earrings. Her curly weave hung in ringlets to her shoulders. Shana was on the prowl for more than a martini and usually Fallon didn't mind playing wing woman, but she was in a sour mood.

"No, you haven't been," Shana said, sipping her drink, "but that's why I asked you to come out tonight. All you do is work and go home to that mausoleum. You are too uptight." Shana looked around the room at the host of men milling around. "Maybe if you met a man and got some good loving, you'd loosen up a bit. I bet I know who could loosen you up while supplying you with the cash influx you need."

Fallon sat forward in her seat. Although she loved her cousin, she doubted Shana, who worked as a hair stylist at a trendy salon, knew much about finance. "Oh, yeah? And who might that be?"

"Gage Campbell ring a bell?"

Fallon's heart plummeted at the sound of his name. "G-Gage?"

"Yeah, you remember him? The guy you had the hots for, for over a decade?"

How could Fallon forget? She'd thrown herself at him and inadvertently set in motion a course of events even she, at her tender age of sixteen, couldn't have predicted. "Of course I remember. What about him?"

"Word in the salon is he's back in town," Shana responded. "A couple of clients have come in talking about dating him. He owns a successful mutual fund business and has become quite the catch. Not to mention, he's still as sexy as when we first saw him when we were eight years old."

Fallon would never forget that day. She'd been prancing around on her pony when Gage and his mother Grace toured the estate with Nora. Fallon had been showing off and the pony had become agitated and thrown her. If it hadn't been for Gage's quick reaction and his catching her before she landed, Fallon would surely have broken something. When he'd looked at her with his dazzling brandy-colored eyes, Fallon had fallen head-over-heels in love with the twelve-year-old boy.

Fallon blinked and realized her cousin was still talking. "According to his current lady loves, he knows his way around the bedroom, if you catch my drift."

There was no mistaking Shana's meaning and Fallon blushed.

"Oh, lord." Shana rolled her eyes upward. "We really do need to get you out if a little girl talk makes you blush. Perhaps Gage could help with Stewart Technologies? I hear he's quite the financial wizard."

"That might be so, but Gage would never lift a hand to help me," Fallon replied. Why would he? She'd ruined his life and she only had herself to blame.

One

Two weeks later

"Stewart Technologies is in dire straits," Fallon told her parents over Sunday dinner.

Thinking about the past and what she'd done to Gage Campbell had weighed heavily on her mind ever since she'd had drinks with Shana a couple of weeks ago.

Fallon had never been able to forget the hateful stare Gage had given her moments before her father had closed the cottage door all those years ago. She'd never learned what had happened to Gage and his mother after they'd left Stewart Manor. She hadn't wanted to know because she'd been the cause of his mother losing her livelihood and the guilt had eaten her up. She'd felt so bad that she hadn't balked when her parents had sent her to a finishing school her final year of high school to avoid her spending time with the "wrong crowd."

"Must you be so dramatic?" Nora Stewart said, glancing at her daughter from the opposite end of the table. Even though it was just the three of them at dinner, her mother had insisted on eating in the formal dining room when Fallon would rather be in the kitchen.

Her mother was the epitome of sophistication, wearing cream slacks and a matching cardigan set. Her smooth chestnut-brown hair was stylishly cut in a chin-length bob while her makeup was perfection. Nora was well-preserved thanks to personal trainers and weekly visits to the salon and spa for massages and facials. Since marrying Henry Stewart and becoming pregnant with Fallon, Nora hadn't worked. *Why should she when she was lady of the manor?*

"I'm not being dramatic," Fallon responded. "We're bleeding money and it has to stop."

"And whose fault is that?" Henry inquired. "You've been CEO for two years now."

When she'd turned thirty Fallon thought she'd finally achieved the height of her career only to find out it had been built on quicksand. Stewart Technologies was leveraged to the hilt all because of her father's poor judgment and her mother's notorious spending habits. Every few years she was constantly redecorating Stewart manor to keep up with the latest fads and, as for fashion, there wasn't a bag, shoe or piece of clothing in her mother's closet that didn't have a designer label.

"Not mine," Fallon said hotly. "Stewart Technologies was in trouble well before I became CEO."

"You're the leader now and it's up to you to fix things. It's what you said you wanted, Fallon," her father replied. "It's time you show what you're made of instead of running to me."

Fallon bristled at that. She'd come to level with her parents, but clearly they were beyond reason. They wanted to stick their heads in the sand and refuse to accept the inevitable: that they were running out of funds and wouldn't be able to live in the style to which they were accustomed. "I have shown my commitment to the company over the last decade. But since it's clear I don't have your support, I'll take my leave." She rose from her seat and made for the door.

"Sit down, Fallon." Her father trained his hazel-gray eyes on her, causing Fallon to pause and retrace her steps.

"If you're going to talk business—" Nora used her napkin to lightly tap the sides of her mouth "—I'm going to make myself scarce because it's such a bore."

Fallon sucked in a deep breath and reminded herself to count to ten, which was more than enough time for her mother to depart. She loved Nora, but she found her exhausting.

"Yes, Father?" Fallon turned and, for the first time, truly looked at her father. She saw more salt and pepper in his normally black hair and a few more lines were etched across his features, showing life wasn't as easy as her mother portrayed.

"I'm sorry if I was harsh before," Henry said. "I know you've been doing your best."

"Which isn't good enough," Fallon stated. "Don't you get it? We could lose everything."

"Surely it's not as dire as you predict?" Henry countered.

"It is. I've exhausted all options," Fallon said. "I even asked Ayden for the money."

Her father's eyes widened. "Why on earth would you do such a thing? He isn't a member of this family. How much did you tell him of our circumstances? What did he say?"

Fallon waited for her father to finish peppering her with questions before answering. Did he wonder if Ayden had told her about his infidelity with her mother? "I was desperate. But I didn't get to explain because he told me he isn't interested in bailing out *our* company because he's not a part of this family." She didn't share that Ayden had had a change of heart and had come to her days ago.

Henry sighed. "It's just as well. We don't need him. You can figure this out, Fallon. There's a reason I let you become CEO."

"*Let me?*" Fallon repeated. "I worked hard to get where I am. I don't recall Dane or even Ayden getting in line to step in your shoes."

"Listen here, young lady—" he began.

"Don't bother chastising me, Father," Fallon interrupted. "I'm the only child you have who cares one iota about Stewart Technologies, so I suggest you stop fighting me and get Mother to understand we are just a few steps away from going broke."

Fallon shot to her feet and, without another word,

left the room, her stunned father sitting with his mouth open at her insolence. She walked quickly to the door and headed for her cottage. Her haven. Her safe place.

The cool night air hit her immediately when she exited. The leaves that had begun falling a few weeks ago crunched under her heels, signaling fall was in full swing. Once inside the cottage, Fallon turned on the lights and sagged against the door. Why was it she felt safe here? The one place that had once caused such misery to others.

Her mother had long since renovated the cottage after the Campbells left. It now had an open concept with a stainless-steel kitchen, sitting area, master suite with en suite bath as well as guest bedroom and powder room. It was all Fallon needed while allowing her to be close to her horse, Lady.

Kicking off her boots, Fallon plopped onto her plush leather sofa, leaned back and thought about the weekend. Once again, she'd scoured the books looking for ways to make cuts and keep the company afloat, but it was pointless. They were going under. And tonight was a complete bust. Her parents refused to accept their new reality: they were broke. The only bright spot had been on Friday evening when Ayden had shown up at her office. He'd looked drawn and tired, and there were lines under his eyes, but he'd wanted to talk. She'd been hard on him because he'd treated her like the enemy for years. She and Dane had been the chosen ones, the children Henry Stewart claimed while leaving Ayden to languish in poverty with his mother.

Fallon understood she'd had the life denied him: the

houses, cars, travel, fancy clothes and schools. He'd listened when she'd explained it hadn't been easy for her, either, with a disinterested, self-absorbed mother and a demanding father who'd pushed her to excel. She was angry that Ayden blamed her when she'd only been a child. However, Ayden had told her he was sorry for ignoring her calls and for turning down her requests for a loan. He wanted to start over, to try to be a family, a brother to her and Dane.

Fallon had been overjoyed. Then Ayden had held her hand and shockingly offered to give *her*—not the company—a personal loan. Fallon knew the sacrifice it had taken for him to make the offer. But, after everything he'd been through, her pride wouldn't allow her to accept his money, knowing how their father treated him. He hadn't supported Ayden as a child. Not to mention she'd had more advantages than Ayden had ever had. She couldn't take his hard-earned money, money he might need one day for his future. He'd nodded and let her keep her pride. And they'd agreed to take baby steps and work on their sibling relationship. Fallon couldn't wait to tell Dane. She hoped he would be as happy as she was to forge a bond with their big brother.

"Welcome back to Austin, old friend," Theo Robinson said to Gage Campbell when they met up for lunch at the country club. They were sitting outside on the terrace by the fire pit, drinking brandy and reminiscing about the good old days.

"It's good to be back," Gage said. And it was. It had been well over a decade since he'd lived in Texas. After finishing college at the University of Texas at Austin, he'd gone on to New York and then overseas to make his fortune. Now that he was a successful man in his own right, he'd come back to his hometown to settle down and take care of his mother. Though he doubted Grace Campbell felt she needed taking care of. Although she'd retired a few years ago, his mother was active and traveled the world with her circle of friends. She deserved it after all the hard work she'd endured to ensure he'd had a future.

"What're your plans now that you're here?" Theo inquired.

Gage sat back in his seat and regarded his friend. "Settle in, find a nice home and a good woman and have some babies."

"Oh, really?" Theo raised an eyebrow. "Since when? I thought you were a die-hard bachelor."

"I was. Hell, I still am," Gage replied. "I'm still indulging until I find Mrs. Campbell."

"Look out, women of Austin!" Theo laughed and drank his brandy.

"There's only one woman who should ever fear me," Gage said, a serious tone to his voice.

"Let me guess. Fallon Stewart? I would think after all this time and your success, you would have forgotten the mistakes made by a young, naïve girl."

"She wasn't so naïve if she had the audacity to show up to my house half naked," Gage responded. He'd never forgotten how stunned he'd been after having a few beers at the bar only to come home to find Fallon in his bed.

"She was sixteen with a crush on you," Theo said. "She was feeling herself, but then her parents caught her. She got scared and lied about what happened."

"Her lies cost my mother her job. And without references from the Stewarts, Mama couldn't find work. It took her months to recover, especially since the Stewarts were paying her minimum wage to work day and night."

"Well, she recovered and so have you. I mean look at you." Theo motioned to him. "You're the wizard of Wall Street. I'd say you've done well."

"No thanks to the Stewarts."

Theo sighed. "Then you'll probably be glad to hear this. The rumor is that Stewart Technologies is leveraged to the max. No bank will loan them money and they've run out of options."

"Serves Henry right," Gage responded. "Though I have to wonder what happened. I thought he had a good head on his shoulders. I even looked up to him once upon a time, admired him when he took me under his wing."

"Henry Stewart isn't running the show."

A knot formed in Gage's stomach. He didn't need Theo to say his next words; he already knew. "Fallon's in charge."

"She's been looking for a handout from anyone she can and has come up empty."

"Is that so?" Gage rubbed his jaw. Fallon Stewart had been taken down a peg and was essentially on the street begging for scraps. Now, if that wasn't karma, he didn't know what was.

"Could be a good time to go in with a consortium and pick up the pieces," Theo stated. "Think about it."

The two men parted right after lunch, but Gage didn't return home to his penthouse at the Austonian in downtown Austin until late evening. It was a temporary oasis with all the modern conveniences a bachelor required. There was a large television with a surround-sound system, an enormous master suite with a king-size bed and a luxurious master bath with room for more than one occupant in the hot tub and massive steam shower.

He went to the wet bar, opened the snifter of brandy and poured himself a glass. He swirled the alcohol around and took a generous, satisfying sip. Sliding the pocket door to his balcony aside, he opened the living room to the oversize terrace with its panoramic views. Austin's city lights twinkled in the distance, but Gage didn't see them. All he saw was a beautiful teenager, wearing the sexiest teddy he'd ever laid eyes on, in his bed. Gage gritted his teeth and forced himself to remember that night. He hadn't just been angry when he'd found Fallon in his bed. He'd been intrigued.

Fallon had been everything he wasn't. Spoiled. Rich. Entitled. She'd had more money than she'd known what to do with, ponies and cars, while he'd worked two jobs. He hadn't wanted to want her, but he had. He'd seen the coy looks Fallon had given him when she'd thought he wasn't looking, but she'd been sixteen. Jail-bait. Gage had been determined to steer clear, but she'd poked the bear and Gage had hauled her against him and kissed her.

If her parents had found them any later, the result might have been him being led off in handcuffs. Instead he and his mother had been shown the door. But now things had changed. He held all the cards and Fallon was on the bottom. He was no longer at the mercy of the Stewarts and whatever scraps they doled out to him. Gage relished how the tables had turned.

Fallon arrived at the Stewart Technologies' offices the next morning feeling out of sorts. She hadn't slept well the night before. She'd been thinking about her lack of a love life. It had been ages since she'd been on a proper date, let alone had a steady boyfriend.

She tried to focus on the day ahead. There were several meetings scheduled, including a negotiation to sell off one of the company's long-held nanotech patents. Fallon didn't want to do it—it was one of her father's significant achievements—but she was running out of options. The cash influx would stave off the bank and ensure thousands of employees kept their jobs.

The morning flew by quickly with Fallon only stopping long enough to eat a quick salad her assistant, Chelsea, had fetched from the deli downstairs.

Fallon was poring over financials when a knock sounded on the door. "Not now, Chelsea, I'm in the middle of something," she said without looking up.

"You don't have time for an old friend?"

Fallon's heart slowed at first and she closed her eyes, leaning back in her leather executive chair. *Surely, it couldn't be.* Perhaps she was imagining things, conjuring up the past. Because she hadn't heard that deep masculine voice in over sixteen years. Inhaling deeply, she snuck a glance at the man standing in the doorway of her office and was bowled over.

It was none other than Gage Campbell.

How? Why was he here at her office? A morass of feelings engulfed her and she tingled from head to toe. The last time she'd seen Gage there had been nothing but hatred in his eyes, not the amused expression he now wore. Fallon reminded herself to breathe in then breathe out.

Calm yourself. Don't let him see he's affected you.

So instead she took the offensive. "What the hell are you doing here?"

Two

"Hello to you, too, Fallon." Gage closed the door behind him and strode toward her desk.

Fallon regarded him from where she sat. Her blood pumped faster as she took in the sight of him. Time had been very good to Gage Campbell. Immaculate and imposingly masculine, he was utterly breathtaking. With his neatly cropped hair, warm caramel-toned skin, thick, juicy lips, bushy eyebrows and those brandy-colored eyes framed by black lashes that always drew her to them, he was impossible to ignore.

He was even sexier than the last time she'd seen him especially with those broodingly intense eyes. He reeked of money and looked as if he was born to wear the bespoke three-piece designer suit, cream shirt with striped tie and polished designer shoes. Fallon knew he hadn't always been this way. The Gage of yesteryear was happier in faded jeans and a wife-beater mucking out stables. The man in front of her was far removed from those days. He stood confident and self-assured.

"I hope I pass the mustard," Gage said after her long perusal.

Fallon blushed at having been caught openly staring and glanced up to find Gage's eyes trained on her. She blinked to refocus. "My apologies. I'm just surprised to see you after all this time."

"I'm sure," Gage responded as he unbuttoned several buttons on his jacket before sitting across from her. Fallon remembered how impossible it had always been to resist those dangerous gleaming eyes of his and today was no different. He looked intriguing, like a total enigma. "It's been what—sixteen years since we last saw each other? You're all grown up." He dropped his gaze and used the opportunity to give her a searing once-over.

Fallon was in her usual work mode. Her naturally wavy hair had been tamed with a flat iron until it lay in straight layers down her back while her makeup was simple: coal eyeliner, mascara, blush and lipstick. Having been blessed with her mother's smooth café-au-lait skin, she required little makeup. And although she was no clothesmonger like Nora, Fallon always managed to be fashionable. She was sporting linen trousers with a sleeveless silk top. She'd abandoned the matching jacket earlier in the day. She wondered what Gage thought of her.

"Oh, yes, you've definitely matured since I last saw you."

Fallon noticed his eyes creased at the corners when he spoke. The sly devil was actually staring right at her breasts and she felt her nipples pucker to attention in her blouse. Immediately she rose. "What can I do for you, Gage? I'm sure you didn't come here for a walk down memory lane."

His eyes narrowed and she could see she'd touched a nerve. "Now that wouldn't be pleasant for either of us, would it?"

Fallon flushed. She'd never forgiven herself for the horrible action she'd taken that had caused his mother to lose her job. She wanted—no, she *needed* to apologize. "Gage, I'm—"

He interrupted her. "I'm here because Stewart Technologies is in financial trouble and I thought I could help."

Her brow furrowed. "And why would you want to do that?"

Gage laughed without humor. "Is that any way to treat a potential investor? Or don't you need an influx of capital to save your father's company?"

"My company now."

"I stand corrected." He inclined his head. "I thought perhaps we could discuss the matter over dinner. My afternoon is rather full and I barely managed to squeeze in this reunion."

"Dinner?" she choked out as she looked at him in bewilderment. Why would he want to break bread with her after their checkered past?

He tilted his head to one side and watched her, waiting for her to speak. "It's the meal commonly eaten after lunch. Or do you have a problem being seen with the former maid's son?"

Fallon looked him directly in his eyes and replied coolly, "Of course not. I'm not a snob."

"Really?"

"You sound surprised."

"If I recall, back in the day you wouldn't be caught dead with me except in the stables or when we were alone."

"That's not true." She felt the flush rise to her cheeks at the memory. "I didn't want us to be disturbed. If my mother found out, she would have forbidden it because..."

"Because I wasn't good enough for you." Gage finished the sentence.

Fallon lowered her head. He was right. It's what Nora had thought. But never Fallon. She'd been too much in love with Gage to see his class or station in life. Agreeing to dinner would show him he was wrong about her and that they were equals. It would also enlighten her as to his true motives.

Several seconds passed and she glanced up to find he'd leaned closer toward her. "Shall I pick you up?"

Fallon shook her head. "No, that's not necessary. I can meet you wherever you like."

"Still not wanting to be seen with me, eh?" Gage uncoiled his tall length, stood and rebuttoned his jacket. A deep chuckle escaped his lips as he made his way to the door. "I'll meet you at the Driskill Grill at seven."

And then he was gone, leaving Fallon to stare at the door. *What was his real agenda?*

Irritation fueled Gage as he headed for the elevator. He was offering Fallon a lifeline and she refused to even allow him to pick her up for dinner! Her arrogance irked him, but so did her beauty. He'd hoped to find a spoiled, selfish shell of a woman, but instead he'd found a stunning and fierce ice princess. Fallon Stewart wasn't the young teenager he remembered. She was a woman. And it angered him that he still found her so…so damned attractive.

When he'd walked through the door and seen her, blood had stirred in his veins and his belly had clenched instantly. He'd wanted to touch her. To refamiliarize himself with her exquisitely soft skin. To crush those sinfully pink-tinted lips underneath his and lose himself. But Fallon had cast her eyes down and acted as if she was unaffected by him.

But the willful sexy teenager who'd come to his bed in the middle of the night wearing nothing but a teddy was still there. Gage was certain he'd seen a spark flare when her eyes traveled the length of him. Now they were both grown and consenting adults, and it was time they finished what they'd started sixteen years ago.

Resolve formed deep in the pit of his stomach. A twist of circumstances had turned the tables and the Stewarts were no longer on top and in a position of power. Gage was. Fallon was exposed, vulnerable and his for the taking. Last night he'd come up with a plan for revenge to finally get back at Fallon and the Stewarts for their treatment of him and his mother.

Stewart Technologies needed cash and Gage was the money man. He not only had loads of it himself, he knew how and where to acquire more. He would convince Fallon bygones were bygones and *help* the company with an influx of cash. Meanwhile he'd secretly purchase stocks until eventually he owned the lion's share and could take it away from them. The best part in this entire scenario was the chance to bed Fallon, the overindulged princess.

Today when he'd seen her, something indefinable had happened. It was as if the years had melted away. Gage had been hit in the gut with the incredible need to possess her. He didn't want any other man to have her, at least not until he'd had his fill.

When he exited the building and slid into the Bugatti waiting for him at the curb, a new idea began to form in Gage's mind.

What if he married Fallon! For his *help* in saving the company, he would become a member of the acclaimed Stewart family and finally not only have Fallon in his bed, but have the prestige he'd always wanted. Because, try as he might, no matter how much money he made, there was a certain echelon of society that still saw him as the maid's son. Wouldn't it get their goat to have him rubbing elbows with the lot of them? To show them he wasn't just the underprivileged kid-made-good? It was a brilliant strategy.

Fallon had no idea what was in store for her tonight.

As he started the engine, Gage's cellphone rang. The display read Mom. "Hey, Mama. How are you?"

"I'd be doing a lot better if you came to see me. You've been back for a while and I've yet to see you."

"I'm sorry. I've been a little busy, and you were away on one of your trips. But I'll visit this weekend."

"Good. It's good to have you back in Austin. It's been much too long."

"Yes, it has." He hadn't been home since he'd finished college and they both knew why. The Stewarts. Gage hadn't thought he'd get a fair break in a town where Henry Stewart had so much power. But the tide had changed, providing Gage the opportunity to put a plan in place to give the Stewarts the comeuppance they so richly deserved.

Fallon didn't have time to go home and change if she was going to be on time for dinner with Gage. A departmental meeting ended later than she'd anticipated, leaving her precious little time to shower in the private bathroom in her office and change into one of several dresses she kept on hand for such occasions. She chose a beaded champagne cocktail dress that accentuated her curves. Refreshing her makeup, she added a touch of blush to her cheekbones to go along with the mascara, eyeliner and pale pink lipstick.

Glancing at herself in the mirror, Fallon felt armed and ready for a night in Gage's company. And she felt like she needed every bit of armor for this unexpected invitation.

Throughout the remainder of the afternoon, Fallon

had wondered why Gage wanted to help her family. She'd come up with only one reason: comeuppance. After the way he'd been treated by the Stewarts, he wanted to be the one to come in on the white horse and save the day. Him, the man her father had thrown out of the house because he'd dared to touch his daughter. Gage wanted them to *owe* him.

Fallon didn't much blame him.

Gage had every right to be angry over how he and his mother had been treated. But now the shoe was on the other foot. The Stewarts were the laughingstock of the business community, turned down by every bank in town because of her father's poor decisions and financial mismanagement. Fallon hoped seeing how far they'd fallen from grace would be enough to salve Gage's wounds.

She made it to the restaurant at seven o'clock on the nose.

The hostess led her to a secluded corner booth where Gage was already seated, wearing a fine, tailored suit. Had he booked this? Did he intend for it to be as romantic as it looked? A dark, quiet corner with a table for two?

He stood when she approached. "Fallon, you're looking lovely this evening." She was stunned when he kissed her on the cheek before she slid into the booth.

"Uh, thank you," she returned, her pulse thumping erratically from the contact of his lips.

"I took the liberty of ordering wine," Gage said, pinning her with his razor-sharp gaze. "A Montoya Cabernet. I hope that's all right?"

She nodded, somewhat amazed at how at ease he was in a restaurant of such wealth and sophistication. He poured her a glass. She accepted and tipped her glass to his when he held it up for a toast.

"And what are we toasting?" she asked.

"New beginnings."

Fallon sipped her wine. "Sounds intriguing."

He grinned, showing off a pearly white smile, and Fallon's stomach flip-flopped. "I've been away in New York and London the last decade. So, get me up to speed, Fallon. How did you end up as CEO of Stewart Technologies?"

"It's really quite simple. My father needed an heir apparent," Fallon said, "and I was the only one willing to step up to claim the throne."

"You make it sound so medieval," Gage responded, tasting his wine.

She smiled. "It isn't that elaborate, I'm afraid. My brother Dane wanted nothing to do with the family business, much preferring his acting career to being an active member of the Stewart family."

"Was it really so horrible growing up in the lap of luxury?" Gage inquired wryly.

Fallon detected the note of derision in his tone. "You'd have to ask him."

The waiter interrupted them to rattle off the daily specials. They both ordered the soup to start, followed by the spinach salad and fish for their entrée. It was all very civilized and Fallon couldn't understand Gage's agenda. Why was he treating her like an old friend when she knew that was far from the case?

Once the waiter left, Gage prompted Fallon. "Please continue with your story, I'm fascinated."

"After what happened between us all those years ago, my father was very unhappy with me."

"Explain."

She sighed softly but didn't stop. "You have to understand, I was his baby girl."

"Dressed like you were ready to take me to bed?"

Fallon didn't rise to the bait. "Seeing me like that made him realize I was growing up too fast and he didn't like it. And I was desperate to regain his affection."

"Had you lost it?"

Gage was perceptive, picking up on what she hadn't said. She didn't answer. "He sent me to a finishing school to ensure I was exposed to the 'right' crowd."

"And were you?"

Her lips thinned with irritation. "They were the snobbiest, cattiest girls I ever met. The teachers were like prison wardens. The entire experience was unpleasant.

"When I returned home, I started accompanying my father to the office and soon I wanted to learn more. My father put me in the intern program and, much to his surprise, I soaked up everything like a sponge. I was interested in learning what it took to run a multimillion-dollar company, so I majored in business. During breaks, I worked at Stewart Technologies, learning the business from the ground up while earning my MBA. Until, eventually, I proved to all the naysayers I had the chops to run the company.

"And, as it turned out, my father was ready to take a back seat. He's now chairman of the board. Of course, I had no idea of the financial straits he was leaving me to tend to. He'd leveraged the business and owed the banks a substantial amount due to projects he'd started but failed to get across the finish line."

"Very intriguing indeed," Gage replied. "And here we are."

Fallon took a generous sip of her wine. She hadn't planned on revealing so much, but Gage was looking at her so intently, as if hanging on her every word.

"And you? Fill me in on your time abroad."

Gage leaned back against the cushions. "I don't think my story is quite as intriguing as yours."

"But it clearly has a happy ending," she replied. "I mean, look at where we are. The roles have been reversed."

"Yes, they have," Gage said quietly. "But I won't sugarcoat it. After my mother and I were kicked off the Stewart estate, she had a hard time finding work, especially because your parents refused to give her a reference."

"Gage…"

"I was young and resilient, with only a year left of college. I worked two or three jobs to keep us afloat. Once I finished school, I struck out on my own. A friend of mine worked on Wall Street and told me I could make a lot of money. The stock market had never really been my cup of tea but, lo and behold, I had a knack for it. From there I went to London, Hong Kong, making money in stocks and foreign trade. Until I settled on mutual funds and started my own business."

"So why come back here?"

"Simply put, I missed home," Gage replied. "I haven't been back since I graduated other than the odd trip. Mostly, I've sent Mom tickets to meet me at some exotic destination. She deserved it, after all her years of menial labor."

Although she'd never experienced the kind of hardship Gage mentioned, Fallon understood his drive to succeed because she shared it.

Over dinner they continued talking about his trading career, lifestyle and trips abroad before returning to the subject of Fallon. It surprised her how easy it was to talk to Gage, considering all that had transpired between them. It felt like a lifetime ago, but she was sure at some point Gage would be getting to the point of the evening.

"Are you having dessert?" Gage asked after they'd polished off nearly two bottles of wine with their meal.

She shook her head. "I couldn't eat another bite." She wiped her mouth with a napkin. "It's been a lovely evening, Gage, but I'm sure that's not the reason you asked me to dinner."

"What do you think the reason is?"

"Payback. What else?" Fallon asked with a shrug of her shoulders. "And although I'm not destitute and put out of the family home, we are in a bind. Surely this must delight you?"

"Not everyone is like you and your family."

Ouch. Fallon took that one on the chin because, after

all this time, he deserved to speak his mind. "Why am I here, Gage?"

Gage leaned forward, resting his elbows on the table and arresting her with his eyes. "I have a proposition for you."

"And what might that be?"

"Marry me."

Three

Fallon coughed profusely and reached for her water glass. Her hands trembled as she placed the glass to her lips and sipped. With all the wine they'd drunk, she must have taken leave of her faculties because Gage Campbell couldn't possibly have asked her to marry him. *Could he?*

"Are you all right?" Gage asked, his voice etched with concern.

"Y-yes." Fallon sipped her water again and placed the glass back on the table. "Can you repeat what you said?"

Gage's mouth curved in a smile. "You heard me, Fallon. Marry me and, in exchange, I'll give you the money you need to save your family business."

She had heard correctly. But he was dead wrong if

he thought for a second she would take him up on his outrageous offer. "Gage! What you're suggesting is insanity! You didn't even give an expiration date for this union. How long would you expect this to last?"

"It's a business deal that will last as long as needed," he stated calmly. "You get the money you need to save a dying technology firm, while I get a wife from an upstanding Austin family. Think about it, Fallon. Our marriage would legitimize my social standing while simultaneously letting all those pesky bankers who have been hounding you know the Campbell/Stewart family is as solid as ever."

"That's real vague. Plus there's any number of society debutantes out there waiting to meet a catch like you, Gage. You don't have to marry me."

"But it's you I want," Gage responded. Within seconds he'd slid closer to her in the booth, until they were thigh-to-thigh.

Fallon flushed. "What are you saying?"

"A caveat to the marriage is it will not be in name only."

"Meaning?"

"Do you really need me to spell it out?" His piercing look went straight through her. "We would consummate the marriage and share the same bed. Become lovers."

Fallon sucked in a deep breath. *Sweet Jesus!* She had drunk too much wine because the words coming out of Gage's mouth didn't make any sense. She took another small sip of water.

"I think we would be quite good together," Gage

said, picking up her hand and turning it over palm side up.

Immediately she tried to pull it back, but his grip was too strong. "How can you say such a thing? I haven't seen you in sixteen years."

"Yet, you still want me." His hold softened but he didn't let her go. Instead his thumb began circling the inside of her palm, making her pulse race erratically. "I can see all the signs of arousal in you, Fallon—the way your eyes dilate when you look at me, the way your breath hitches when I come near. Even the way your breasts peak with one look from me."

Fallon felt her cheeks flame. Was she so obvious that he could read her like a book? It was as though he'd put her under some kind of spell, the same as when she'd been sixteen. And why oh why wouldn't he stop circling her palm with his thumb? He was teasing her and she didn't like it. She jerked her hand free. "Stop it, Gage."

"Stop what?" he asked so innocently she would have thought he meant it, but she knew better.

"Whatever game it is you're playing."

"No games. Just facts. I'm willing to give you millions to help Stewart Technologies, even though it's been hemorrhaging money. I'm willing to give my money to help save your company. And in return, I offer you the chance to be my wife. I think it's a fair trade."

"Of course you would." Fallon scooted out of the booth. "But I'm not a stock to be bought and traded. Furthermore, you got your signals wrong. I'm not interested in you in the slightest." She made it as far as the foyer of the restaurant before Gage caught up to her and swung her into a nearby alcove.

"You're not interested in me, eh?" Gage asked, stepping closer into her space. So close, her body was smashed against his. "How about we test that theory, shall we?"

She saw the challenge in his eyes seconds before his head lowered and he sealed his lips to hers. Fallon wanted to refuse him but the thrill of having his lips on hers again was too much to resist. Need unfurled in her, the likes of which she hadn't felt since…since the last time he'd kissed her. No other man had ever come close to making her feel this way.

This hot. This excited.

Gage's arm slid around her waist to the small of her back and he pressed her body even closer to his. Meanwhile his tongue breached her mouth, allowing him to increase the pressure, demand more and compel her to accept him. The kiss was hard yet soft, but also rough enough to thrill her. Fallon's lips parted of their own accord and his tongue slid in. Teasing, stroking, tasting the soft insides of her mouth.

Fallon whimpered and her stance relaxed as the sheer power of his kiss enflamed her. Sliding her arms around his neck, she held his head to hers, reveling in the deeply carnal kiss. Gage ground his lower half against hers and she felt every inch of his hard body. Her tongue searched his mouth ravenously and he met her stroke for stroke. Her breasts rubbed against his chest and her nipples hardened. Fallon had never felt so desirable and could have gone on kissing him, but Gage pulled away first.

His breathing was ragged but he managed to say, "I've proven you are interested, but I'll give you some time to think about my offer."

Fallon looked up, dazed and confused. "Wait a minute." How could he compose himself after that kiss? "How much time?" she croaked out.

"Forty-eight hours."

She shook her head. "I can't make a decision about the rest of my life in two days."

"Well, that's too damn bad because that's my offer," Gage responded. "You can take it or leave it. It's up to you." He tapped the face of his Rolex watch. Then he reached inside his suit jacket and pulled out his business card. "My personal cell. Call me when you're ready to say yes."

A whirlwind of thoughts swirled around Fallon's mind as she somehow managed to drive herself home from her dinner with Gage. When she got back to the cottage she kicked off her heels, undressed and removed her makeup, and put on her old college T-shirt. Sliding into her king-size platform bed and falling back against the pillows, Fallon recalled the bombshell Gage dropped.

Marry me.

Gage had proposed marriage in exchange for saving Stewart Technologies, the company her father started forty years ago. Could she let it slip through her fingers without a fight? But Gage wasn't offering a marriage in name only. He wanted them to become lovers.

The thought both excited and terrified her, especially after that hot kiss at the restaurant. Her attempt to appear unaffected had been smashed to smithereens. The chemistry between them was off the charts. He'd smelled and tasted so good. And the way he'd held her close, her heart had fluttered unlike anything she'd ever felt with other men. Had his one life-changing kiss all those years ago ruined her for anyone else? Because there hadn't been many men. Since Gage she'd never succeeded in finding someone who could fulfill an ache. So instead she focused on her career at the expense of her personal life. Work was her baby, so much so she hadn't given much thought to marriage or children.

Would Gage want children?

No, no, no. She shook her head. She wouldn't have children with a man as part of a business arrangement or for money like her mother had. She was no fool. She knew Nora hadn't married her father for love. Instead she'd married him for the life he could give her. Fallon wouldn't want that for herself or for Gage. And why would he want to marry her anyway? She'd lied and cost his family their livelihood. He should hate her but instead he was offering her a way out. It didn't make sense. He could be setting her up for failure so he could give her the comeuppance he thought she deserved.

Was she honestly giving Gage's proposal serious consideration? She couldn't. Shouldn't. He'd been a brute, only giving her forty-eight hours to make a life-changing decision. Marry him or risk losing the company. Marry him and agree to be his wife, *his lover*. He could have been her first if they hadn't been interrupted by her parents. Fallon remembered the passion she'd felt in his arms then and now. Was it fate they would end up in this predicament? Was she always destined to be his?

Unable to sleep, Gage restlessly prowled his penthouse. Wondering. Wishing. Hoping.

Would Fallon say yes?

Would she agree to marry him?

He knew it was wrong to give her an ultimatum but he'd had to. Once she committed, he didn't want her to change her mind. When she agreed to be his and his alone, they would have a quick engagement, a big splashy wedding and a satisfying honeymoon. He wanted the entire community and all of Austin society to know *he*, the maid's son, had bagged Fallon Stewart, heiress to Stewart Technologies. He would rub it in all their faces that the young man they'd bullied because of his humble background had turned into a successful and wealthy entrepreneur.

Fallon *needed* to agree. She wasn't going to get a better offer. She'd exhausted every avenue. No one was going to lend her the amount of money required to turn the company around. A personal gift from him to Fallon would ensure Stewart Technologies stayed viable. In the meantime, since most investors were ditching shares, he would gobble them up until he owned the majority interest. Once he owned enough shares in the company, he would ensure it turned a profit or he'd die trying.

The best part of the deal was that he would finally take Fallon to bed. It was long overdue and very, very necessary. Tonight, when they'd kissed, he'd nearly combusted. She'd tasted exquisite and he remembered how her nipples had turned to stiff peaks against his chest. He'd wanted to break through the icy barrier she'd erected and find the passionate girl who'd stolen into his bedroom. And he had. When she'd opened her mouth to let him in, he'd taken all she'd had to give. He still had a thick, hard erection to prove it. If they hadn't been in a restaurant, Gage would have ravished her where she stood. But he was no animal. He was willing to wait. Hell, he'd waited nearly two decades to *be* with her—another few weeks wouldn't make much difference.

Four

"He did what?" With a look of shock on her face, Shana sat back on the couch in Fallon's cottage the following evening. She'd arrived a half hour ago. After the pleasantries were over, Fallon had uncorked a vintage bottle of Merlot and gotten right down to the matter at hand.

"There's nothing wrong with your hearing, Shana," Fallon replied. "I was just as floored as you were."

"When I mentioned Gage the other day, I was trying to get a rise out of you. I never dreamed he'd ever loan you the money let alone ask you to *marry* him. It's crazy!"

Fallon nodded. "I thought the same thing."

"Thought?" Shana peered at her strangely. "As in past tense?"

"Yes. But after considering it—and trust me, I couldn't sleep a wink last night—it kind of came to me."

Shana's eyes grew wide. "What came to you?"

"It makes an odd sort of sense in a way," Fallon responded. "Gage has always wanted to be part of the *in crowd*, but growing up on the estate, he was always thought of as the help. Marriage to me would be a way for him to even the scales."

"And make you pay on your back."

"Shana!"

"C'mon, doll." Shana scooted closer to Fallon on the sofa. "Don't tell me Gage didn't make a play for you. You're a grown woman now and a beautiful one, I might add. There's no way he's not trying to tap that." She patted Fallon on the behind.

"My God, Shana. Have you no shame?"

"Do you? Because it sounds to me like you're giving Gage's offer some serious thought."

"Wouldn't you?" Fallon asked. "A sexy, gorgeous, *rich* man is offering to solve my financial problem and save my family. How can I let the company fail under my watch?"

"See?" Shana pointed her index finger at her. "That's how he got you. He's tapping into all your fears and insecurities. Let it fail, Fallon. You didn't create this mess, your father did. You inherited it. And now you're supposed to—what? Give up your chance of finding Mr. Right and settle for Mr. Payback? Because that's exactly what this is. Mark my words. Gage wants revenge for how your family wronged him and he's using all the weapons in his arsenal."

"You make it sound like we're at war."

"You are. Think about all the anger, hurt and humiliation he must feel after *you* threw yourself at him and caused him and his mother to be kicked out on the street. The man must despise you, but clearly he wants you in equal measure. It's all kinds of messed up."

"You're not helping me, Shana."

"I have always been a straight shooter, Fallon," Shana replied. "It's what you love about me, so I'm telling you how I see it. I want you to consider what you could be getting yourself into before you make a life-altering decision."

"Aha!" Fallon said. "You've given me an idea."

"Oh, yeah? What's that?"

"If I agree, I can stipulate the marriage is temporary. I think six months is enough time to get Stewart Technologies back on its feet with an influx of cash and cement Gage's place in Austin society. What do you think?"

Shana shook her head. "I don't know, Fallon. You're playing with fire."

"Without risk, there can't be a great reward." Fallon sure hoped she was right because she was banking her future and Stewart Technologies on making the right call.

Gage couldn't wait forty-eight hours for Fallon to make a decision. He had to persuade her. All day in his home office he'd been thinking about her and he knew the only way to stop himself from going crazy was to see her again.

He picked up his cell phone and called her.

"Gage?" Fallon said. "Have you changed your mind? Did you come to the conclusion your arrangement was just as crazy as it sounds?"

"Quite the contrary. I wanted to *see you*."

"You told me I had forty-eight hours."

"And you do," Gage replied smoothly. "I'm going to do everything in my power to convince you to say yes. Starting with a date tonight."

"Tonight? I can't. I have to work."

"Excuses, excuses, Fallon. You're afraid to be alone with me after what transpired between us last night."

"That's not true." She paused for several beats. "I admit I find you attractive."

"Face facts, Fallon, if we hadn't been in public, the evening might have ended differently."

"You're very sure of yourself."

"I know what I want."

"And…oh, that's right, you want me," Fallon finished. "Well, I'm not that easy, Gage."

"I didn't think you were, but I admit I'd like to know more. Last night was the tip of the iceberg. Let me see you tonight."

"I need time to think, Gage. I don't appreciate the strong-arm tactics."

"I would think if you're going to agree to shackle yourself to me, you would want to get to know the man you'll marry. Or would you rather walk into this as strangers?"

"You seem to think it's a forgone conclusion I'll say yes to your outrageous proposal."

"I'm encouraged because you haven't said no."

"Fine. I'll meet you. Where and when?"

Gage shook his head. Oh, no, he wasn't falling into this trap again. He wanted a proper date. "*I* will pick you up at Stewart Manor. And, Fallon?"

"Yes?"

"Dress to impress. Because I'm taking you to the opera."

Gage ended the call with a smile on his face. That hadn't been as hard as he'd imagined. She was recalcitrant, but he'd convinced her it was in both their best interests to get to know one another. The problem was he didn't have tickets, but he'd heard from Theo that Puccini's *La bohème* was playing at Austin Opera and he knew anyone who was anyone would be there.

Austin society would see the former maid's son out on the town with Fallon Stewart. It was brilliant. He would kill two birds with one stone. Cement his place in society and spend time with the woman who would be his wife. Now he had to convince Fallon there was no way she could walk away from him.

Dress to impress.

Fallon stood in front of her gilded pedestal mirror and glanced at the double-strapped, off-the-shoulder red gown with a deep side slit. The dress showed a generous amount of leg while the sweetheart neckline revealed a swell of cleavage.

She didn't want to give Gage any ideas that the evening would end differently than it had last night with them each going home *alone*.

After applying some red lipstick and a touch of blush to her cheeks, she was ready for an evening at the opera. *But was she really ready?* The remainder of the afternoon after Gage's call, she'd picked up the phone to cancel a half a dozen times. Yet she'd always stopped herself because maybe deep down she really did want to see him.

Fallon couldn't understand the pull Gage had on her after all these years. He'd awakened something in her and she wasn't sure how to get it back under control.

The doorbell rang and her stomach lurched. There was no turning back. Grabbing her matching red clutch purse and wrap, she made for the front door. When she swung it open, Gage stood there, resplendent in a black tuxedo with satin lapels. He was wearing a red tie that complemented her dress.

Fallon felt his eyes rake her up and down. It made her feel as if she was plugged into an electrical socket because currents were running through her veins. When she looked into those brooding brandy-colored eyes, her insides hummed.

"You look incredible!"

"Thank you," Fallon said coolly and wrapped her shawl around her shoulders.

Gage took her arm and led her outside to the waiting limo. He helped her inside, picking up the hem of her dress as she slid in.

Once he was seated beside her and the chauffeur closed the door, he reached across the short distance to the ice bucket and pulled out a bottle of Dom Péri-gnon. He uncorked it easily and poured them a glass. He handed her one and dinged his flute against hers. "To an unforgettable evening."

Fallon was sure it was going to be nothing but.

La bohème was everything. Gage had spared no expense. When they arrived, they were shown to box seats near the front of the opera house with a clear view of the stage. The singers were amazing and, by the end of the night, Fallon was on her feet along with the entire theater giving them a standing ovation.

"I didn't realize you were such a fan," Gage said from her side.

"I've come from time to time with my father," Fallon replied. "Mama couldn't be bothered. Said it was much too boring for her, but I loved it. Plus, it was something my father and I could do together."

"Must be nice," Gage said wistfully as he led her out of the theater and away from the throng.

"Did you know your father?" Fallon asked, turning to give him a sideward glance.

Gage's glare told Fallon she'd made a misstep in asking something so personal. Wasn't the point of tonight's exercise for them to get to know each other?

Their limousine was waiting by the curb. Fallon was thankful they didn't have to wait with the crowd lining the streets. Within minutes they were pulling away and Gage asked the chauffeur to raise the privacy screen.

"Where to next?" Fallon inquired. There had been an uncomfortable silence between them since she'd inquired about his father. It was clear Gage didn't wish to speak of him.

"I didn't know him," Gage said finally.

Fallon didn't need to ask what he meant.

"My mother never spoke of him. Only told me that he was an older gentleman who'd taken advantage of her youth and naïveté. Once she was pregnant, he turned his back on her and she never saw him again."

"That's why you pushed me away," Fallon replied softly. "Because you didn't want to be like him."

When Gage turned to her, his eyes were cloudy. "Very insightful of you. But know this, Fallon. If you had been a few years older, I wouldn't have turned you away."

"You wouldn't?"

"No. I would have taken what you offered."

"Why?"

"Because I wanted you. I wanted you *then* and I want you now."

His face was starkly beautiful in the dim light coming from the street and Fallon felt as if she were being hypnotized. Her hand went to her throat. Her mouth felt parched as if she'd walked hours in the desert with no water to hydrate her. She reached for the champagne bottle; a new one had miraculously appeared.

Gage grasped her arm and a tingling went straight to her core. "Does it scare you when I speak so openly?"

"You mean bluntly?"

"I was being honest. You should try it."

Her eyes flashed with anger. "I have been honest. I'm here with you now, aren't I? When every instinct

I have tells me I should be running in the other direction, away from danger."

"You think I'm dangerous?"

"Hell, yeah! But I can't…"

"Can't what?"

"Can't seem to stop myself from wanting you, too. How's that for honesty?"

"It's great because I've been craving your sweet mouth all day," he growled. Within seconds he'd slid her along the seat until she was sprawled across his lap. The air around them was heavy and thick with desire. When Gage trailed a finger down one of her cheeks, Fallon felt her pulse beat hectically at her throat. "I know you don't want to want me, Fallon, but your body betrays you." With one arm securely around her waist, the other hand was free to cup her jaw and, with a surprising gentleness, Gage angled his head and his mouth closed over hers in the most persuasive of kisses.

Tender yet insistent, his mouth claimed hers again and again and her lips clung to his, seeking closer contact. Fallon gave herself permission to enjoy the taste and lush depths of his mouth. Gage gathered her to him, his fingers at her jaw, holding her captive as he lazily explored her mouth. His tongue teased and stroked hers, causing heat to pool low in Fallon's belly and spread like wildfire, incinerating everything in its path. Her breasts felt heavy and swollen. Gage sensed her ache and cupped the underside of one breast. His thumb grazed over the nub until it peaked and hardened.

Fallon moaned, loving the delicious yet tormenting strokes of his fingers. She wanted his mouth on her nipple, wanted him to feast on her. She became dimly aware of Gage pushing down the top of her dress and taking the rigid peak in his mouth. His mouth and tongue worked the nipple with licks, flicks, tugs and suction. The ache inside her intensified when Gage transferred his attention to her other nipple.

Hadn't she known they might end up like this? This was no longer about a kiss. It was about need. And now that the desire had been unleashed, she didn't know if it could be bottled up again.

Gage ran his hands down Fallon's body. Touching her in ways he'd imagined for far too long. Of course, now that he had her exactly where he wanted her, his brain had short-circuited. He was hardening underneath her sweet little bottom, and he was completely useless. All he could think about was how he'd love nothing better than to wrap her legs around his hips and take her right there in the limousine.

And her breasts. God, they tasted heavenly. It made him want more. He moved upward so he could slant his mouth over hers again. He loved the hot slide of her tongue in and out of his mouth and the way her hands clutched his tuxedo jacket as if she was seeking something to hold on to. But there was nothing. Nothing but this white-hot arousal between them. His free hand went up and undid her hair, which fell to her shoulders. Gage slid his hands through the tendrils and cupped the back of her head so he could give her another mind-numbing kiss.

But a kiss wasn't all he wanted. His hand moved

lower until he came to the slit of her dress. He hiked it up to her waist and moved his hands up her bare legs. She trembled when Gage's finger found her thong and pushed it aside so he could trace the most intimate part of her. She was so wet for him. Her body was betraying her, showing him physical evidence of her arousal. And when he began to circle the top of her clitoris with a feather-light touch, she gasped. When he slid one finger inside her, her body tightened around him.

Gage watched Fallon's face as he worked her with his fingers. Slowly, deliberately, he brought her higher and higher. The sounds of pleasure she was making, and especially the way she writhed against his hand, turned him on. Her sexy bottom was brushing his erection and he was going mad. He added another finger and her eyes became hazy with passion.

"Come for me, Fallon," he commanded. She closed her eyes and he sensed her resistance, but his hands were insistent. He could feel it when she orgasmed and clenched around his fingers. Satisfied, Gage claimed her mouth with his, whispering his approval as aftershocks shuddered through her entire body. He kissed her through them until she eventually quieted.

Fallon's uninhibited response was more than Gage could ever imagine. Now he realized *he* needed her to say yes because they were far from over. In fact, they'd just begun.

Five

Fallon was embarrassed as she came back down to earth and registered what had happened. She'd allowed Gage to make love to her in the back of the limousine. Her breasts were bare, aching and wet from his mouth, while her dress was pulled down to her hips. Did he think she behaved this way with every man? Well, she didn't!

She quickly scrambled out of his lap to pull her dress up over her breasts and push it down her thighs.

"What's wrong?" Gage asked.

"How can you be asking me that? After I— After we—"

"Behaved like two consenting adults?"

Fallon flushed and moved as far away on the

seat as humanly possible without falling out of the limo.

"Tonight was inevitable, just as it's inevitable that we'll become lovers. Marriage agreement or not."

The limo stopped and Fallon realized they'd made it to her cottage. She was thankful when the door opened and she was out in the cool evening air, briskly walking to her front door. Unfortunately she was not alone. Gage followed her.

"I'd like to walk you to your door."

Fallon spun around on her heel, "Oh, no, you don't." She held her hand up against his hard chest. "We'll say our good-nights here."

"All right." Gage handed Fallon her wrap. "You might want this."

"Thank you."

"Good night." He started back toward the limo but then turned around. "About tomorrow…"

"I'll call you," Fallon responded.

"Very well, I'll await your answer." He'd slipped inside and the limo took off down the gravel driveway.

Once inside, Fallon grappled with how the situation with Gage had escalated. One minute they were enjoying the opera and the next she was coming apart in the limo. How was it possible they still shared such a passionate connection after their storied past? Whenever he was near, she felt weak, fluttery and out of control. Her feelings for Gage had always been complicated, but adding sex into the equation would make it a hell of a lot harder to walk away from a marriage. Was she honestly considering going through with it and locking herself in unholy matrimony with Gage?

Yes.

The next day Fallon was as jittery as ever. She had a hard time focusing on work as the clock tick-tocked. The forty-eight-hour deadline Gage had given her loomed. And she couldn't get the man out of her mind or the way she'd burned up for him with every kiss and every caress. She was unnerved at how far things had gone. She was thankful it hadn't gone any further. She didn't need full-blown sex clouding the picture when she had such a momentous decision to make.

On the one hand, Gage was offering her a way out. It would save thousands of jobs and allow her employees to keep food on the table. She would show her father and all the naysayers that she had the expertise to run Stewart Technologies. On the other, marrying Gage and agreeing to his nonnegotiable terms would mean consummating the marriage. If she agreed, all the old feelings she'd once had for Gage could come bubbling back up to the surface, making her vulnerable. Because could she really trust him, given their history? And she doubted he trusted her, so what was in it for him?

She was reading through some reports when her baby brother, Dane, swept into her office and swung her out of her seat into his arms. "Fallon! Baby girl, I've missed you."

"I've missed you, too, you big oaf. Now put me down, so I can have a look at you." She hadn't been expecting a visit from him, but then again Dane danced to the beat of his own drum, doing things in his own way and his own time. "What are you doing here? I didn't know you were coming for a visit."

When Dane finally set Fallon on her feet, she peered up at him. Dane had inherited their mother's dark brown eyes instead of their father's hazel-gray ones like her and Ayden. His classical good looks, tawny skin, chiseled cheekbones and smile had won the world over, making him one of America's favorite actors. Today he was dressed casually in Diesel jeans, a black T-shirt and biker boots, and was rocking a serious five-o'clock shadow like he hadn't shaved in days.

"When did you get in?" Fallon inquired, leading him over to her sitting area.

"An hour ago, but I'm not staying long. I decided to lay over here for a couple of hours on my way to Mexico for a movie shoot."

"Dane? You promised me that the next time you came to town, you'd stay for a spell."

"I'm sorry, sis, but we have a tight schedule," Dane responded, flopping down on her sofa and putting his booted foot on her cocktail table.

Fallon came forward and knocked it off. "Have you forgotten your manners out there in LA?"

Dane grinned mischievously. "Not all of them. But I had to come. You sounded down the other week when I called, so I had to see for myself what all the ruckus was about. Everything looks the same."

"That's because I've been keeping the bankers at bay."

Dane frowned. "And now? Are they threatening to

take the house? I think Nora would have a fit if she lost her gravy train."

"Must you call our mother by her first name?" Fallon replied.

"C'mon, Fallon," Dane said, "When has that woman ever been a mother to us? She was always pawning us off to a nanny or maid. Well, that was until you ran off the one good maid we had."

Fallon felt her face flush and cast her eyes downward. She wished Dane hadn't brought up Grace Campbell. It was still hard remembering how Fallon's actions had affected not only Gage but his mother, as well.

"Fallon." Dane scooted over on the couch and grabbed her hand. "I'm sorry, okay? I didn't mean to stir up the pot and bring back bad memories. Anyway, I realize I've been out of commission and on the sidelines in this family, but I know money is tight. How much do you need? I can liquidate some assets and get you probably a couple of million in a few days."

"It wouldn't be enough."

Dane's dark brown eyes grew large. "It's that bad? Why didn't you tell me? I could have been helping instead of frivolously spending on houses, cars and trips."

"It's okay." Fallon patted his hand. "I didn't want to bother you. And, furthermore, it's your money. You earned it."

"But I'm your brother. I want to help."

"Ayden offered to help, as well."

"Ayden? Wow!" Dane shook his head. "I'm still in shock over your call. After all this time, he wants a relationship with us? Do you know why?"

Fallon shrugged. "Does it matter? We're family."

Dane was noncommittal. "Sure. And I can see how important it is to you, so I'll make the effort. All right?" He tipped her chin up to look into her eyes.

Fallon grinned. "Great! I'll plan something soon for the three of us."

"What are you going to do in the meantime about the company?"

"Don't you worry, your big sister always has a plan."

Why wasn't she here yet? Gage paced his penthouse like a panther stalking its prey. Fallon had called him earlier and asked to meet at his place, so he'd given her his address. And waited. But the call had been over an hour ago. Gage wondered if Fallon didn't want to be seen with him. Is that why she was coming to him? Did Fallon want to keep their association a secret from her family? Was she having cold feet?

He went to his subzero refrigerator and pulled out a beer. Unscrewing the top, he took a generous swig and slid open the sliding pocket doors to the balcony.

Gage was certain she would agree to his terms. Why else would she bother coming? If she wasn't interested, she'd have laughed in his face when he'd first made the offer and told him where to go. But she wouldn't. Not after last night. They'd given in to the fiery passion be-tween them. And now she was coming to him. She'd be on his turf. *Did she know the danger she was in?*

Gage found himself wondering what it would be like when they were finally together. When there were no parents standing in their way or terms to discuss.

Just a man and woman in the throes of passion. Blood rushed to his head and his groin, making him both dizzy and hard at same time. He still couldn't wrap his mind around why she affected him this way. It mocked everything he'd ever said about what he'd do to Fallon if he ever saw her again. He thought he'd throttle her for her careless behavior, but instead all he wanted to do was to drown himself in her. She was the key, the final piece to achieve all he'd ever wanted.

He already had money and power, but by marrying Fallon he would have the grudging respect and acceptance of society. He would no longer be living in the shadows and envying the Stewarts' charmed life, which had been utterly different from his humble roots. Instead he would be living it with them. But, unlike the Stewarts, he wouldn't take what he had for granted because he knew what it was like to go without.

The sound of his doorbell forced Gage from his thoughts. With a loose-limbed stride, he walked to the door and opened it.

Fallon was wearing a black sheath with a sharp asymmetrical collar. Her hair was pulled up into a high bun and she wore little to no makeup. She looked effortlessly beautiful. Gage yearned to touch her but her features were schooled.

"Come in." He motioned her forward.

"Thank you." She walked inside and paused when she reached his living room. It was large, with sweeping views of the capitol building and the University of Texas tower. "Great view."

"Yeah, I like it," Gage replied. "But I'm sure you

didn't come here for the scenery. Have you made a decision?"

Fallon eyed him warily. "Yes, I have. But I have a few stipulations that aren't open for negotiation."

Gage chuckled to himself. *Did she actually think she was in a position of power?* He held all the cards and he was damn well going to play them. But he would humor her. "All right, let's hear them."

"I'll agree to marry you."

His mouth curved into a smile. Of course she would. She was desperate to save her father's legacy. Was that her only reason?

"But only for six months."

"Excuse me?"

"Six months is enough time for you to ingratiate yourself into Austin society and get the full benefit of the Stewart name and all its connections. I see no reason for us to continue the charade a moment longer than necessary. Wouldn't you agree?"

Gage had to admit he was surprised; he hadn't thought of making their arrangement temporary. The only thing on his mind was Fallon in his bed and getting a foothold into Stewart Technologies. "I can live with that. What else? Because I suspect there's more."

Fallon stood straighter and stared at him. "The marriage must be in name only."

Gage laughed. "Do you really think that's possible, Fallon, after the way you were crawling all over me last night?"

"I—I…" She stuttered but then stopped. It appeared as if she was regrouping. "I don't want to muddy the waters and complicate what is essentially a business arrangement. You must see that."

"No, I don't." Gage plopped his beer on the nearby cocktail table, causing some to spill over. "What I see is a woman afraid of taking what she wants. You and I know this isn't just about business, Fallon. It never was."

Her eyes narrowed. "What is it?"

"It's a reckoning. Between you and me. About what we both wanted but didn't get years ago. Don't you think it's time we find out what could have been?"

Fallon turned and walked onto the terrace. She was quiet, contemplative, as if she were battling herself, and Gage feared she would say no to him. It was imperative she agree. It would finally give him the means to avenge his mother while simultaneously getting Fallon in his bed.

Gage touched her shoulders and she jumped. Rather than touch her again, he placed his hands on either side of the railing, closing her in. She was out of options. He heard her sharp intake of breath as he inhaled the sweet fragrant smell of her perfume. "Fallon…"

"All right," she whispered.

Gage sucked in a breath and leaned in closer. "Say it again."

"I said, all right." Fallon turned around to face him and he appreciated how she looked him in the eye. She was no coward. "I'll agree to the stipulation we share a bed."

Victory surged through Gage and a large grin spread across his lips. "Then how about we get a head start."

He hauled her to him. He was following his base instincts of taking her here and now. He didn't care. On the couch or his bed, it didn't much matter to him. She was his now. He lowered his head to finally have a taste of her delectable lips, when Fallon placed her hands against his chest.

"No."

"No?" Fallon made him feel a little wild and out of control while she still looked poised. "You said that you were agreeing to my terms."

"And I will." Fallon slid out of his grasp to walk back into the living room. "When we're married."

"You expect me to wait until our honeymoon?"

Fallon chuckled. "As shocking as that sounds, yes, Gage. You've called the shots up to this point, but not on this. I'm agreeing to marry you and to share your bed, but not until then."

Gage gave her an eye roll and sighed. Fallon played hardball and was a shrewd negotiator. He could see now how she'd climbed the ladder to become CEO of Stewart Technologies. "Fine."

"Good." She inclined her head. "I assume you'll have your attorney draw up a prenuptial outlining terms, including your *gift* to your fiancée?"

"Of course. The prenup will state the exact amount of funds I'm giving you to bail out your company. Other matters will be between us—a gentleman's agreement, if you will."

"Excellent."

"And as for the wedding, it needs to be arranged quickly yet lavishly so the entire community can see it."

"Why the rush?"

"You need a reminder of our explosive chemistry? Then let me remind you." He slipped his arm around her nape and covered her mouth in a searing kiss. She was stiff at first, but it didn't take long for her to warm up and to delve into the kiss. He angled his head for better access and reveled in how Fallon tasted like no other woman. Over the next six months he intended to get rid of this craving he'd developed for her.

His hands skimmed down her back to cup her bottom and she groaned. Jesus, if he continued, he would have her flat on her back despite her protests. Gage pulled away and took a shuddering breath. "You should go now while you still can."

"I think that's a good idea." Fallon grabbed her purse and was out the door, leaving only her scent in her wake.

Oh, yes, they needed to have a very short engagement.

Six

"Gage, darling. It's so good to see you." His mother enveloped him in a warm hug. Gage returned her affection, squeezing her small frame.

He pulled back and regarded her. She wore a simple shift-style dress and espadrilles, and looked youthful. The earlier years of hard menial labor couldn't be seen in her smooth caramel complexion. Her dark brown eyes were warm and inviting, reminding him he had been away from home far too long.

"C'mon in." She motioned him inside the five-bedroom palatial home he'd bought her a decade ago when his finances had begun booming. Gage had ensured that his mother could retire from a life where she worked late into the night cleaning other's people houses and looking after their children.

"The place looks great." Gage followed her into the sunroom where she had set a pitcher of sweet tea and her famous oatmeal-raisin cookies in the middle of the cocktail table. Gage snatched one from the platter and began munching away happily as they sat on the sofa.

"The interior decorator you hired had a great eye. Once I told her I wanted modern contemporary, she came up with this." Grace motioned to the sleek white furniture and the room mostly done in creams and light beige with a few colored throw pillows here and there. "Now, let me pour you some sweet tea."

"Good, you deserve it." He accepted the glass when she handed it to him.

"Tell me what's new. You must have something on the horizon. You wouldn't leave your precious London otherwise."

Gage shrugged, not meeting her eyes, and reached for another cookie. "Why don't you tell me about your next trip?"

His mother eyed him suspiciously and Gage squirmed in his seat. "Don't play with me, boy. Your mama can tell when you're not being forthright. So spit it out."

Gage sighed. He would have to tell her about Fallon, but he didn't relish her response. "I ran into an old friend recently and we reconnected."

"Really?" His mother poured herself a glass of tea. "Anyone I know?"

"Fallon Stewart." Gage didn't look up when he spoke. He didn't need to because the silence permeating the room was deafening.

"The Stewart girl who caused me to lose my job of

ten years without so much as a reference?" his mother responded. "What in hell's name is going on, Gage? I thought you despised that family as much as I did."

"I do but…"

"But what?" Her fierce gazed rested on his. "Explain yourself."

Gage wasn't sure how much of his plan he wanted to tell his mother, so he gave her a half-truth. "She's turned into a beautiful young woman."

"She's deceitful. Had Fallon Stewart spoken up years ago, she would have saved us years of struggle."

"She apologized and wants to move on."

"And you've forgiven her?" his mother asked incredulously. "After you vowed vengeance? I can hardly believe that."

"Believe it, because Fallon and I are getting married."

"What?" Her eyes grew wide. "Over my dead body."

"Mama, don't be melodramatic."

"I'm not. That girl is your Achilles' heel, Gage. She always has been. I remember how she used to fawn over you and follow you around like a little puppy dog and you never put her straight. And now you're turning the other cheek? Sounds to me like you're thinking below the belt and not with your head."

Gage reached across the sofa and grasped his mother's hand in his. "I know what I'm doing."

"Do you?" She gazed deep into his brown eyes. "Because I think the Stewarts will do nothing but destroy you. Mark my words. You're playing with fire, Gage."

"Trust me, Mama, I have the situation under control." *Or did he?* Was he blinded by Fallon's charms and headed for a fall?

"I don't think so, but then again you're a grown man and capable of making your own decisions."

"I'm glad you recognize that because I will make them pay dearly for how you were treated. I promise you." He would take sweet revenge on Fallon. In bed.

"Let me get this straight. After I told you the Stewarts' company was in trouble, you thought it would be a good idea to confront Fallon?" Theo asked when he and Gage met up to play pool late Saturday afternoon.

"Yeah," Gage responded. "I had to see for myself if she was still the spoiled, overindulged princess she once was."

"Well, apparently not, because you asked her to *marry* you," Theo said, taking a swallow of his beer. "Have you lost your mind?" He leaned over to feel Gage's forehead.

"No. I haven't," Gage said. "Fallon's not sixteen anymore, Theo." He used the cue stick to get the green ball into the corner pocket. Then he eased the cue into position for the blue ball and aimed for the middle pocket. He missed and it was Theo's turn. "She's a grown woman."

"Then sleep with her," Theo stated. "You don't have to marry her. I mean, I know she's hot and all." He glanced over at Gage and laughed when his best friend gave him a jealous glare from across the pool table. "Hey, I have two eyes, I'm not blind. But since it's clear you're the possessive type, I'll keep my opinions to myself."

"You do that."

"Answer me this. I get why she's doing it. You're offering her a ton of money to save her business and you two have a history, so I understand the attraction. But what do you get out of all this, because a bed partner seems like a flimsy excuse to tie yourself to another human being in holy matrimony."

Gage reached for his beer on a nearby table. After telling his mother, Gage had been shaken. But on his way over to meet Theo, he'd had to remind himself of why he was doing this and his resolve strengthened. "I told you. Fallon will secure my place in society and while she's so busy focused on the wedding, I'll be secretly buying up stock of Stewart Technologies until I own a majority interest."

Theo pointed at him. "I knew you had a trick up your sleeve, but this is pretty underhanded, even for you, Gage."

"Don't you think they deserve it?" Gage countered. "Henry Stewart threw us out on the street with just the clothes on our backs. We weren't even allowed to get our meager belongings. And after working for them for years, they wouldn't even give my mother a reference. All because she stuck up for me." He slammed his hand against his chest. "Do you know how the guilt ate me up at causing my mother harm?"

"I know it wasn't easy."

"It was hell. We had to scrape by with the little savings we had. I blame the Stewarts. And I will feel triumph the day I can ruin them."

"And Fallon. Even though she was a naïve young girl?"

"She was old enough to know better and she's no young ingénue anymore. She's well aware of what she's agreed to."

"She's not the only one," Theo responded. "I worry about you, Gage."

"Don't. I've been on a collision course with the Stewarts for sixteen years and the moment has finally come for me to get vengeance. And after telling my mama, I'm even more convinced I'm doing the right thing."

"You told your mother?"

Gage nodded. "And she pretty much blew a gasket."

"Can you blame her?"

"No. But I'm on track to get everything I ever wanted, including Fallon."

This marriage was one of the best decisions he'd ever made and the unexpected bonus was the sizzling sex awaiting him once he finally made Fallon his. He wasn't going to let up on the gas. Gage had to push forward until he took over the Stewarts' empire. Only then would he feel like he had avenged his mother.

Fallon was happy to receive a lunch invitation from Ayden. She arrived before him on Monday afternoon and had several minutes to settle her nerves. Their meeting would be very different from the tense scenario a couple of months ago. Fallon would get to know

Ayden on a personal level. She didn't know why she was nervous at the prospect, but she was. She wanted this so bad and it had meant everything that Ayden extended the olive branch.

She noticed her big brother the moment he arrived. He was over six feet tall, bald with tawny skin, and impressively male in his tailored suit. He was impossible to miss. He waved when he saw her and stalked toward the table. His eyes creased into a smile and she was surprised when he leaned toward her and offered a hug. They were off to a good start.

"Sorry I'm late. A client meeting wrapped up later than I anticipated," Ayden said as he sat across from her. "How are you?"

"I'm good. Thank you for the invite." Fallon glanced over and found herself looking into the hazel-gray eyes they shared with their father.

"You're welcome," Ayden responded, unbuttoning his suit jacket and leaning back to regard her. "When I said I wanted a relationship, I meant it."

Fallon nodded and smiled. "I know. So did I."

"So, in the interest of family, I'd like to know how you're really doing. Any luck on getting a financial bailout with any of the banks I referred you to?"

After he'd told Fallon he wanted to forge a sibling relationship, Ayden had sent her some leads. As owner of Stewart Investments, Ayden's clients were quite wealthy and might be looking for an investment vehicle.

"No, I didn't get any bites," Fallon responded, reaching for her sparkling water.

His gaze bore into her. "What are you going to do then? You're running out of time."

"I've found a private investor."

Ayden frowned. "Who would have that kind of cash?"

"Gage Campbell. You may have heard of him."

"Yeah, I have. They call him the Wizard of Wall Street. But usually he's making other people money, not investing his own." He peered at her with a strange expression. "What gives?"

"Gage and I have a personal connection," Fallon replied, forcing her eyes to meet her brother's. "And…" She tried to find the right words but it was hard with Ayden staring at her so intently. She could lie. Spin it that they were old acquaintances. But Ayden wouldn't believe it. And she didn't want to start out their newfound relationship that way. She had to tell him the truth. "We're getting married. And in exchange, Gage is giving me the money to bail out Stewart Technologies." Fallon shot Ayden a glance, but his eyes were blazing with fury, which stunned her. She didn't know Ayden cared.

"Marriage?" His eyes widened in concern. "Why would you agree to such a thing? I will *give* you the money. You don't have to marry this man."

She shook her head. "It's all right, Ayden. I've known Gage for years. We grew up together. And…"

"And what does he get out of this arrangement?" His eyes narrowed as he waited for her answer.

Fallon blushed and he caught it. "So you're willing to pros—"

Her eyes flashed a gentle but firm warning. "Don't you say it, Ayden, not unless you want this relationship to end before it's begun."

She heard his sharp intake of breath and his eyes were hooded when he spoke next. "You're my sister, Fallon. A fact I've been trying to hide from a long time but not anymore. I'm responsible for you taking such drastic action. I made you feel like you had no other choice."

Fallon leaned across the table and placed her hand over his large one. "Listen, I appreciated your offer. Ultimately it was my choice, Ayden. Not yours. You're not responsible for my actions."

"And you're not responsible for Henry running the company into the ground, especially after he frivolously spent money on new inventions that never went to market," Ayden responded hotly. "Yet you're willing to sacrifice yourself."

"Please respect my decision," Fallon implored. "I need your support on this."

Ayden sighed and sat back in his chair. "I'm worried for you."

"Don't be. I know Gage. He won't hurt me." Fallon certainly hoped that statement was true because she wasn't only risking her pride. Gage had the power to hurt her more than any other man because of the long-ago buried feelings she had for him. She had to protect herself at all costs. She might be giving her body, but not her heart.

Fallon was exhausted. It had been an emotionally draining day. All she wanted was to go home and soak in a long, luxurious bath. So much had happened in the last couple of days. Dane and Ayden were both so concerned for her well-being she needed to regroup, to make sure she could handle what she'd signed up for.

Seeing Gage again and finding out the passion she'd once had for him hadn't died but blossomed was disconcerting. Over a decade had passed. He should no longer cause her pulse to race, but he did. She was a bundle of tight emotions and lust. Whenever she was in his company she acted completely out of character, starting with the heated kiss at the restaurant then again in the limo after the opera.

Is that why she'd agreed to his marriage proposal? He was a rich and successful man with deep pockets that could help save her company, but was it more than that?

Her phone rang and she answered it from her car. "Fallon?"

"Gage. What can I do for you?"

"I'm here at Stewart Manor and thought you'd like to join me."

"You're at my house? Why?" Panic surged through Fallon. *What was he doing there?* They hadn't even had time to get their story straight. And then it dawned on her: he couldn't wait for the opportunity to rub it in her parents' faces. He was marrying their daughter. It was a *take that* to her father. It would serve him right if she told Gage to go to hell, but then she would still be in the same predicament tomorrow.

She heard his chuckle from the other end. "I thought

it would be obvious. I'm here to share the news of our impending marriage with your parents."

Fallon sucked in a sharp breath. "You had no right to do that. *I* was going to tell them."

"*We* are going to talk to them, so meet me here." The call ended and Fallon glared at the display screen. Anger coursed through her and she let out several choice words. Who did he think he was, running roughshod over her? She had been planning to tell her parents in due time. What right did he have to force her hand like this?

Apparently, in his view, every right. He wanted to be able to rub the fact they were getting married in her family's face. The maid's prodigal son had returned and was there to save the day. This was all part of his retribution. She could only imagine what her mother's response would be: sheer and utter embarrassment at having to kowtow to Gage Campbell.

She was wrong.

After parking her red Audi in the circular driveway, Fallon walked into the manor expecting to hear loud voices, but she found Gage and her parents lounging on the sofa as if they were fast friends instead of known enemies.

She caught Gage's compelling stare the moment she entered the room. With his height and broad shoulders, he was beyond handsome. The words that came to mind were *potent*, *vital* and *commanding*. Fallon found herself mesmerized.

"Babe." Gage rose and strode toward her, a barely leashed tension radiating off him. He leaned forward and brushed his lips across her temple before circling his arm around her waist. Fallon allowed herself to be ushered to the sofa where they sat side-by-side, thigh-to-thigh.

"Fallon, darling." Nora was perched in a chair opposite her father while she and Gage sat on the sofa between them. "Why is this the first we're hearing that you've been seeing Grace's son?"

Fallon was vexed. The innocuous question made it seem as if Nora and Gage's mother were old friends rather than boss and employee with a bad history. She didn't get a chance to respond, though, because Gage was quick to answer.

"We were keeping it private, Mrs. Stewart. We reconnected some months ago." He turned to Fallon at his side. His eyes, fringed with long black lashes, held hers for several seconds before he faced her parents again. "We didn't want to let the cat out of the bag, so to speak, until we were sure of where the relationship was heading."

"But Fallon never keeps anything from me." Her father glanced in her direction.

Fallon attempted a half-hearted smile. "I'm sorry, Daddy."

Gage reached for her hand, which she'd kept firmly in her lap, and laced his fingers through hers. "Don't apologize, Fallon. We wanted privacy. Besides, it doesn't matter now. We're in love and we want to get married as soon as possible."

Nora gasped. "Why the rush? You aren't pregnant, Fallon, are you? I mean, what would everyone think?"

The horror in her mother's voice over the idea that *she* would get knocked up by Gage of all people was clear to everyone and Fallon felt Gage stiffen at her side. She patted his leg and answered. "Of course not, Mother. We see no reason to wait. We're both very eager to tie the knot."

"Perhaps it would be best if you had a long engagement." Henry eyed them both. "It would give us time to get to know Gage again."

Gage looked at her father. "Oh, I'm sure you know me quite well, Mr. Stewart, considering I grew up in this household and you took me under your wing."

Fallon's stomach plummeted and her father bristled.

Her mother spoke first. "That may be so, Mr. Campbell, but—"

"Gage," he interrupted. "I mean, I am going to be your son-in-law, after all."

Fallon watched her mother plaster on a fake smile. "Gage, it's clear you've done quite well for yourself…" she began. Fallon knew her mother had noticed his Tom Ford shoes, Rolex watch and tailored designer suit, but did she have to be so *obvious*? "But we really know nothing about you."

Gage leaned back against the sofa, one arm draped casually behind Fallon. "Well, after my departure from Stewart Manor, I went on to graduate from the University of Texas with a degree in finance and economics."

"You were always a whiz with numbers," her father said.

Gage continued as if he hadn't spoken. "After college, I went to work on Wall Street, then in London and Hong Kong, where I made a number of substantial investments that have put me in the position I'm in today."

"And where is that exactly?" Her mother pursed her lips. "As you can see—" she swept her arms across the room "—Fallon has grown up in a certain lifestyle and we wouldn't want her to do without."

Gage's eyes narrowed as he sat forward. "As my wife, Fallon would want for nothing. Money is no object for our wedding."

Her mother's finely arched eyebrow rose. "No object, did you say?"

"That's right."

"Well then, Henry." She turned to her husband. "Seems like our daughter has landed quite the whale. Having Gage here—" she inclined her head in his direction "—should most assuredly fix the company's dire straits."

"Mother, please."

"It's all right, Fallon." Gage patted her thigh. "I'm aware of the company's financial problems."

"And will you be assisting in that effort?" Henry responded. "Or is this all a ploy to get back at me? Do you even love my daughter? Because I'm finding it very hard to believe, after all these years, you're willing to let bygones be bygones."

Fallon could tell Gage was seething with rage. He slowly stood. "The time for me justifying myself to you, Mr. Stewart, is long since over. I suspect it's you who should be thanking me for even considering jumping onto this sinking ship." He buttoned his suit jacket.

"Fallon?" He glanced down at her. She had no choice but to stand, as well. "If you'll excuse us."

"Wait just a second, Campbell." Her father jumped up. "I'd like to talk to my daughter *alone*."

"So you can talk her out of marrying me?" Gage asked with eagle-eyed precision. "I don't think so. Fallon is coming home with me."

Fallon looked at her father and then back at her fiancé. She could feel the hostility emanating from both men and realized she was caught in the middle *again*. If she went with her father, he would surely ask questions she wouldn't want to provide him the answers to. She had to go with Gage because she needed to lay a few ground rules on how this engagement and marriage were going to work. Gage couldn't have everything his own way. He would have to give.

She nodded her acceptance and Gage placed his hand at the small of her back and ushered her out of the room.

Seven

Gage fumed as he and Fallon strode toward the front door and he didn't say a word as he walked her to his car. He'd known facing the Stewarts after all this time wouldn't be easy. He'd hoped to get some satisfaction at seeing the shocked expression on their faces, but he hadn't expected the rage that had grown deep in his gut with each passing moment. Perhaps he shouldn't have been hotheaded and waited for Fallon. He'd been on edge because his mother had called him earlier and tried to talk him out of the marriage. He'd had to do something big so *he* wouldn't change his mind.

Once they made it to his Bugatti, Gage opened the door for Fallon and she glared at him. "Is this really necessary? I can go home. I'm right here."

"Yes, it is. Get in."

Fallon must have thought better of arguing with him and slid inside the vehicle. He closed the door behind her, came around to the driver's side and started the car. He didn't need to look at his passenger to know she was angry with him.

Once they pulled away from the estate, she turned to him. "There was no reason for you to behave like a caveman back there. My father gets we're together. He didn't need to know you were taking me back to your place."

"I had cause."

"You rose to the bait," Fallon said.

It galled Gage that she was right. He should have acted as if he couldn't care less about their disdain, but instead he'd shown his hand. "Your father needs to know I won't be pushed around, not again."

"Well, neither will I, Gage," Fallon replied, folding her arms across her chest. "I agreed to your terms, but I don't take orders from you or anyone. You got that?"

Gage glanced at her sideways. Fallon had guts and he liked that about her. Not to mention those luscious, ripe lips of hers. He felt himself getting hard.

"The light changed," Fallon commented.

Gage glanced up; indeed it had. He slid the car forward. "I'm sorry if I was a bit *heavy-handed.*"

Fallon eyed him narrowly. "An apology? Wow! I'm surprised you could manage it."

"I can admit when I'm wrong." He heard her mumble something underneath her breath. "What was that?"

"Oh, nothing," she said. "Since we're going to your place, I hope it's your intention to feed me because I'm starved. I was looking forward to a meal and a hot bath."

Envisioning Fallon naked underneath a sea of bubbles was quite the erotic fantasy. "Both of those can be arranged."

"I'll take the meal now. Bath time will be later at my cottage alone."

"Damn." He snapped his fingers. "I was hoping you might want some company."

"Not a chance, Campbell. If you recall, our agreement was to wait until after the wedding."

"C'mon, don't tell me you're not tempted. I give great back rubs."

"I bet you do. Now, drive please."

"With pleasure," he replied.

When they made it to the penthouse, he started for the kitchen. He tossed the jacket he'd been wearing aside and rolled up his sleeves to rustle up some steaks and a salad for dinner. He noticed how Fallon made herself comfortable in his home and he liked it. She busied herself, taking off her jacket, kicking off her heels and following him into the kitchen. He watched her pull two wineglasses from the cupboard and a corkscrew from a drawer. Then she went over to the wine rack nestled in the living room corner and pulled out a bottle of his favorite red wine. Clearly she was as on edge as he was as she quickly set about opening the bottle. He stopped her.

Taking the corkscrew from her hands, he uncorked the bottle and poured them both a glass. Fallon moved over to the sofa and drank in silence while he prepared dinner.

"I'm sorry about my parents," Fallon said after some time had passed.

"Why are you apologizing for them?" Gage asked as he placed the steaks in the microwave to thaw and turned on the broiler.

"Because…"

"Just stop, Fallon." She had no idea what it was like to escape the dead-end world he'd grown up in. To claw his way out, inch by painful inch, to make something of himself. To achieve the heights he hadn't thought he could. And to have her parents look down on him angered Gage. Henry didn't think he was good enough for Fallon. Nora was a different story; as long as Gage kept their bank account flush, she was content to pawn her daughter off. It disgusted him. But Gage reminded himself of his end goal. Bed Fallon. Take away Henry's most prized possessions—his daughter and his business—and leave him with nothing.

He gathered the fixings for a salad from the refrigerator and began cutting up the vegetables.

"You sound as if you're angry at me," she said softly, turning to face him from the sofa. "It was your decision to go off half-cocked. I would have told my parents on my own. In *my own time*."

"And when might that have been? On our wedding day?" he asked, taking the steaks from the microwave and liberally seasoning them.

She shot him a penetrating glare. "No, but you jumped the gun and now you're mad because you didn't like their reaction. Well, tough! You didn't give me time to set the stage. You went in guns blazing. If you'd given me time for a little diplomacy, I could have smoothed the waters."

"There's no time for diplomacy, Fallon," Gage said, placing the prepared salad in the fridge until the steaks were done. "They were never going to approve of you marrying me. What's done is done. They know. We set a wedding date." He placed the steaks in the broiler.

"Christ! Can you let me catch my breath?" Fallon implored.

No! he wanted to scream. If too much time passed, she could change her mind or his mother would change his. It was imperative the train left the station. He'd already contacted his attorney last night and told him to prepare the paperwork.

"I'm sorry if I'm being pushy here," Gage said, finally answering Fallon's question, "but I see no reason to delay the inevitable. I would think you would welcome a swift engagement and wedding to secure Stewart Technologies."

Fallon flushed. "Of course I want that. I just…" Her voice trailed off and she took a sip of wine.

"Just what?"

"Nothing." She reached for her purse on the cocktail table and pulled out her cell phone. "What date were you thinking of?"

"October first sounds great. A fall wedding would be brilliant."

"That's a month away!"

"I know, but your mother can help," he responded. Nora Stewart loved spending money. Although he wanted a big splashy wedding, he would have to keep Nora on a short leash because she was a notorious spendthrift. Did it really matter anyway? In the end, he'd have his way. Fallon in his bed.

"You still seem worried about the wedding," Gage said a few minutes later when they were seated for dinner.

"I have a lot on my plate right now." Fallon glanced down at the steak and spinach salad with a balsamic vinaigrette Gage had prepared. "No pun intended."

They both laughed. "How'd you learn how to cook anyway?" she inquired. She wasn't much of a cook herself and was surprised at Gage's talent. She told him so as she cut into her perfectly cooked steak.

"From my mom," Gage replied. "She didn't always have time to cook for me if she was at the main house. Some nights I had to fend for myself."

Fallon was quiet. She'd never thought about what happened to Gage when Grace was cooking all their meals. "I'm sorry, Gage."

"For what?"

Tears welled in her eyes and she said, "For everything. For how I treated you back then. For not thinking about you when your mother was at the house catering to mine, to me and Dane. I—I guess I didn't care about anyone else but myself back then. And I'm sorry."

Gage stared back at her, his expression unreadable, but Fallon wasn't stopping. She owed him this and it was long overdue. "I'm sorry I lied about you to my father and accused you of seducing me when we both know it was untrue. I was afraid. I didn't know what my father would do after he caught us. I didn't want to disappoint him and the way he was looking at me frightened me. I was afraid of losing his love."

"I doubt one mistake would have cost you his affection."

Fallon lowered her head. "Maybe. Maybe not. I'm trying to give an explanation for why I did what I did."

Gage stopped eating and watched her warily. "I'm listening."

"All my life I tried to be the son he never had because he and my brother were like oil and water from the day Dane was born. I knew Daddy wanted a son to follow in his footsteps, so I tried to be that person. Then one day I learned Dane wasn't Daddy's only son. He had an older son, Ayden, from his first wife, Lillian."

"I heard rumors Henry had another son. The papers alluded to it when they were covering Ayden Stewart of Stewart Investments, but he would never confirm it."

"Because Ayden hates our father. Wants nothing to do with him. Blames him for the awful childhood he had growing up."

"And you?"

"He knew of me, but I was the one who made contact with Ayden when I was eighteen. I was in college and away from my parents and wanted a relationship with the big brother I never knew existed."

"What happened?"

"Ayden wasn't interested in being a family and I accepted that. But things have changed. He's ready to put the past behind us and be siblings." Fallon didn't share that initially she'd gone to Ayden for help but upon further thought had realized she wasn't being fair to him.

She couldn't ask Ayden to save a company he'd been cut out of. She'd agreed to Gage's marriage proposal and that's all that mattered.

"Then I'm glad for you," Gage replied. "I wish I had siblings growing up when I lived on the estate. It would have made it a lot easier to deal with the bullies. We could have double-teamed them. Instead it was just me. But eventually I grew up. Got taller. Stronger. And no one dared to approach me."

"Until the day a sixteen-year-old stole into your cottage and ruined your whole life," Fallon responded.

Gage glanced at her. "Fallon, I thought we agreed to let this go."

Like her father, Fallon had her doubts. She didn't want to be played. "So you've said, but I just poured out my guts to you and yet you haven't said whether you accept my apology."

"I accept. There, are you happy?"

"Only if you mean it. If you truly mean it."

"I can accept, but it doesn't mean I've forgotten. Is that fair enough for you?" Gage inquired.

Fallon nodded because she suspected she wasn't getting any more blood out of that stone. "All right. Now, about this wedding. You realize you told my *mother* you want something lavish."

Gage pursed his lips. "True. I'll meet with my accountant and we'll give her a substantial budget for the wedding. But in general you need to get her spending under control or you'll never stabilize the company."

They continued talking finances until they retired to the living room and killed off a second bottle of wine.

At some point Gage swung her legs into his lap. He closed his hands around her heels and began massaging her feet. His long fingers slid from her heels to her toes as he encompassed them in firm, sure caresses. Fallon allowed herself to relax and rest her head back against the sofa. The slide of his hands against her skin felt so unbelievably good. Warm, gentle…and erotic.

"Mmm…that feels good," Fallon moaned as Gage used his thumb and fingers to hit the pressure points.

"My pleasure," Gage murmured. "Can you make that noise again?"

Fallon popped an eye open and caught his sly grin.

"C'mon, you must recognize how sexual that moan was," he said. "And I'm a man, after all." He pressed his fingers against the soles of her feet and Fallon's body arched off the sofa. "A man who's attracted to you."

Fallon straightened and wondered frantically how she'd got herself into this. When she looked up, she found him watching her intently. Desire had been awakened in the dark depths of his eyes; they glittered in a way that unnerved yet excited her, speeding up her pulse. She moved to turn away, but Gage wouldn't let her up. Instead he leaned forward. Her hands pressed into the silk of his shirt. She felt the solid wall of his chest and the rapid thump of his heartbeat.

She tried to push him away but somehow her fingers had a mind of their own and instead slid along his arms, molding his incredibly muscled biceps. Sensation coursed through her and she was transfixed as he lowered his head and kissed her with a thorough slide of his lips against hers. They traded kiss for kiss and

Fallon clasped his face in her hands and angled her head for deeper contact. Gage plundered every inch of her mouth and she gave him full access.

How was it they always managed to end up here? Like this?

From her sensual fog, reason emerged. Then caution. If she allowed herself, she'd get caught up in the fervor because when they were together like this, Fallon was certain Gage had forgiven her and the past was long behind him. But she was afraid to allow herself to believe it. As he'd said, he'd accepted her apology but hadn't forgotten what happened. It would always be between them.

Fallon pressed her hands against his chest and Gage stilled. He must have sensed her pulling back since he stopped and was already on his feet. She saw him rub his head in frustration.

"I think it's best if I leave." Fallon reached for her purse behind her on the console and stood. "We should refrain from spending too much time alone together until the wedding. I'm going to call an Uber."

"Fallon, you don't have to do that. I can drive you home."

She held up her hand. "Please, let me have some time alone, okay?"

"All right, all right. We'll talk soon?"

"Of course." Fallon knew Gage would make sure of that. He'd staked his claim not only on her but on her body. And if she didn't get some distance between them there was no way they would remain celibate until after the wedding.

Eight

"Care to tell me why you're marrying the house-keeper's son? A man who nearly assaulted you years ago?" Henry Stewart stood at Fallon's office door the next morning wearing a dark gray suit and a scowl.

"Daddy, what are you doing here?"

"I'm here to find out what the hell is going on." Her father closed the door and headed straight to her plush sofa.

Fallon released a deep sigh. She'd known this day was coming, but it was here. To move forward, she had to tell the truth about what really happened when she was sixteen.

"You have it all wrong, Daddy." Fallon came from behind her desk.

"What do I have wrong, pumpkin?" He patted the seat next to him.

Fallon sat beside him and looked into his hazel-gray eyes. "When I told you Gage came on to me, I lied. It was the other way around. I came on to him and *he* pushed me away."

"What?" Her father's eyes grew large with concern. "Why on earth would you do such a thing? Grace Campbell was good people and I threw her and Gage out on the street."

Fallon bowed her head and smoothed the pale pink dress she wore. "I know. And I've never forgiven myself for the pain I inflicted on their family. But in that moment I panicked."

"I see. And is this marriage some sort of penance? Because you feel like you owe him? Well, guess what? You can't make up for the past, sweetheart."

"It's not like that." She shook her head. "Gage and I...well, like he told you before, we've reconnected."

"If that's code for you slept together, I don't want to know." Her father bolted to his feet. Then he spun back around quickly. "But if you did, why marry? Although Gage may not be the scoundrel I thought he was, he still has to harbor resentment. There has to be more to the story because this is all too sudden."

Fallon wasn't going to explain the conditions under which she'd agreed to marry Gage. She'd already done enough to disillusion her father for one day. "There is no catch, Daddy. Gage and I are getting married and you'll have to accept it."

"I have to do no such thing. Gage Campbell isn't good enough for you, Fallon. I hope you see that before it's too late."

Gage hadn't seen Fallon in a week. He was anxious. The prenup was ready—his lawyers had couriered it over just this morning—and he wanted her to sign it before she changed her mind.

Although he'd agreed to her request for some space, it had been much harder to honor than he'd anticipated. Far too hard. Business was no longer paramount in his mind even though his attorney told him they were close to acquiring a big round of Stewart Technologies' stock through several different obscure holding companies. It would take someone months to discover that he owned all of them. It should make him feel good that he was achieving his goal to squash the Stewarts, but it didn't. His mother was disappointed he would even consider "marrying the enemy," as she put it. He'd tried to explain that he had a plan, but she would hear none of it.

Today, however, he and Fallon would cement their relationship by meeting for lunch at Capitol City, Austin's most exclusive country club. It was a blatant statement they were together and would certainly start the rumor mills churning. For privacy, he'd reserved the entire terrace for just the two of them. He glanced down at the manila envelope that held the paperwork formalizing the agreement between them. It was all in black-and-white. It laid out the monetary gift that would help her keep Stewart Technologies, some of the terms of their marriage, and the fact they'd each keep their individual assets in the event they divorced. Now all Fallon needed to do was sign.

He glanced at the entrance to the terrace. Fallon walked in wearing a simple navy sheath with a deep V, and desire flared hot in his belly. She smiled at him when she approached and he couldn't stop himself from grinning. She had a tantalizing figure with her long, shapely legs and pert breasts. His pulse quickened. He couldn't wait to find out firsthand how she would come apart when he had her underneath him.

Gage rose and schooled his features as he prepared to finally make Fallon his.

Fallon paused by the terrace doorway. The last week away from him had been good for her equilibrium. She'd been able to get her rampant lust for the man under control by explaining it away. Gage was a skilled lover. He knew how to seduce women and, given her limited dating experience, she'd been pulled into his web.

She wished her explanation to her father had gone equally as well. It hadn't. When she'd finally spoken with him after the night of their announcement, he'd been less than pleased, but Fallon had stood her ground. She'd even gone further and told him she was putting him and her mother on a budget. Stewart Technologies would no longer fund their lifestyle and their expense account would be shut down.

Her father had been furious and told her she had no right to do such a thing, but as CEO she had every right. Although he was chairman of the board and still had shares, Fallon wasn't going to kowtow to him anymore. She had the board on her side. Henry hadn't been pleased, claiming Gage was asserting undue influence over her, which was ludicrous. Fallon was finally doing what she should have done years ago when she'd been appointed CEO and realized the dire situation the company was in.

Meanwhile her mother was in serious spending mode. She'd already recruited Austin's top wedding planner to organize their hasty nuptials. She wanted to sit down with Fallon and go over color swatches, flower selections and cake choices, but Fallon wasn't interested. She'd told her mother whatever she selected was fine. Knowing her mother, it would not only be flashy, but lavish enough to appeal to Gage and ensure he got his money's worth because he wanted everyone in Austin to know he'd landed the golden goose. Her.

When she arrived at the table, Gage helped her into her seat. "Thank you. You're looking well," she commented when he sat across from her.

"And you're looking good enough to eat," he responded, placing his napkin in his lap.

Fallon noticed the amused expression on his face and realized how formal she'd been. Then she noticed the envelope on the table. "I take it that's the prenup."

"Yes."

"Hand it over." She held out her palm.

"In time. Let's have a drink." A waiter came forward and, after taking his wine order, departed. "We need to milk this." He inclined his head toward the window of the club dining room where several sets of eyes were watching them from inside.

She plastered a smile on her face. "Of course. I know how important appearances are."

His eyes narrowed. "Yes, they are. If you recall, that's one of the benefits of marriage *for me*."

She'd offended him, but it was too late to take it back now. "I'm well aware of the *mutual* benefits of this marriage. You don't have to remind me."

"Good."

The waiter returned with the wine and poured them each a glass. They both ordered the seafood entrée and the waiter left, giving them the privacy Gage craved.

Fallon didn't wait for a toast. She quickly took a long sip of her wine. She noticed Gage staring at her. "What?"

"Are you nervous?"

"Why would I be?" she asked tartly. "I'm just agreeing to bind myself to you, a man I hardly know, for the next six months."

"You didn't mind being with me last week." He drank some of his wine.

"How gentlemanly of you to remind me," Fallon answered. "We may not have a problem in that department, but I would have preferred it if we could have kept this strictly business."

"I'm sure you would," Gage responded, "but it's because of our *personal* connection the opportunity to save your company is even possible." He slid the envelope toward her. "You'll find everything is in order as per the changes requested by your attorney."

"You've already signed," Fallon commented as she flipped through the pages.

"I know what I want." The smoldering flame she saw in his eyes shouldn't have startled her, but it did. Fallon swallowed the frog in her throat.

"It appears in order. I should have my attorney review it one more time."

"That's a stalling tactic. Sign it, Fallon."

Her eyes flashed fire. "Don't bully me, Gage."

"We made the changes he requested, you can see for yourself. I want this settled between us." Gage sipped his wine again, watching her over the rim of his glass. "As you know, I don't have the full amount you need sitting in a bank account. I need time to make it happen. The sooner I get started, the better."

"You make it sound so easy. It's not." If she did this, there was no turning back. She would become Mrs. Gage Campbell and all that entailed, in and out of his bed. It was overwhelming. She sucked in a deep breath.

As if sensing her unease, Gage went in for the kill.

"If you don't sign, it's only a matter of time before you go belly-up. Think about all those lost jobs. It's a win-win for both of us, Fallon. Sign the document." Gage pulled a pen from the inside pocket of his suit jacket and handed it to her.

Fallon looked down at the pen in her hand for several beats. He was right. The sooner they got this over with, the better. Lives depended on her decision. She had to get the company back on its feet as soon as possible and Gage wouldn't turn over the money until Fallon walked down the aisle. Then, and only then, would Stewart Technologies be in the black.

Fallon scribbled her signature on several pages, slid the document into the envelope and handed it back to him.

"I imagine you should feel relieved," Gage commented.

"Not in the slightest." Her feelings for Gage were intensifying and now she'd agreed to marry him, to share his bed for six months. She feared for her heart because she could easily fall for him as she had in the past. And would he want her if she did? Gage had agreed to a temporary marriage of convenience. For him, they would be completing their unfinished history because, really, that's what this was. Somehow she would have to maintain her dignity.

"Be relieved," Gage suggested. "We're a team now. No matter how crazy life gets, you'll have me to rely on at least for the next six months."

"You make it sound so easy."

"There's no time for doubt or second-guessing, Fallon. It's done. Don't tell me you're not up for the challenge?"

"Of course I am," Fallon retorted.

Gage surprised her by reaching across the table, threading his fingers through hers and placing a kiss on them. "I promise you. We've got this."

Gage was on his way to the Stewart Technologies' barbecue the next Saturday to make an appearance as Fallon's fiancé. He was in the clear to attend because

Henry had long since retired from coming to company functions, allowing Fallon to spearhead them. Now that the paperwork was signed, Gage felt like he was back in the driver's seat because he understood what was at stake. He doubted Fallon did.

She'd taken a calculated risk in accepting his offer without really understanding his motivations. His hatred of her family went deep. Deep enough he would do anything for revenge, including marrying the woman who'd started it all while secretly buying up shares of her company. Her apology for her actions had come a little too late in his opinion. For years all he could see was red and now he had the Stewart family right where he wanted them. Dependent on him.

My oh my, how the tables have turned, Gage thought as he pulled his Bugatti into a parking space at Mayfield Park. Stewart Technologies had rented the park for the company event, which would include food, games and prizes. He wore his favorite pair of faded designer jeans, a T-shirt and sneakers since they were experiencing a sort of Indian summer.

From the large cloud of smoke coming from several enormous grills and smokers, Gage could see the barbecue was already underway. There were large arrays of delicious fixings—including beans, macaroni and cheese, greens, potato salad and coleslaw—covering the large rectangular tables. At least two hundred people were milling around and getting involved in various activities. Men were on the football field while women played cards at a picnic table. Children tossed

Frisbees or horseshoes. Quite an event to pull off for such a large group of people.

Gage was impressed by Fallon's managerial skills and her generosity, because Fallon was sponsoring the event from her personal finances. He found the lady of the hour passing out lemonade. It made his mouth water—not the delectable drink, but the outfit Fallon was wearing. She had on a crossover halter top showing off her sleek shoulders and buff arms while her cut-off jeans hugged her behind. Gage wanted to growl in protest because every man here could see what would soon be his.

Fallon turned around at that moment and saw him. She wiped perspiration off her brow. "Can you believe how warm it is today?" she said, smiling. "Would you like some lemonade?"

"I'd love some." He needed something to quench the desire that overtook him at seeing her half naked. She handed him a cup and he damn near guzzled the entire thing.

"Easy," she said, laughing. "You'll want to stay hydrated. Hey, Laura," she yelled to a woman standing nearby, "can you take over for me for a while?"

"Sure thing, boss."

Once Fallon came out from behind the table, he wasted no time circling her with his arm and giving her an openmouthed kiss right in front of the entire table. When she pulled away she said, "What was that?"

"A proper hello."

She grinned and he allowed her some distance. "So,

what do you think?" She motioned around the park. "Pretty awesome, huh?"

"You really know how to put on an event."

"Walk with me a minute." She surprised him by shoving her arm through his and leading him away from the group. Was it for his sake or their audience's? Because several people had watched their kiss. "I know you probably think we don't have the money for this, but morale has been at an all-time low. The employees heard rumors. They think we're going to fold. I want them to know we care."

"You mean *you* care," Gage corrected.

She gave him a sideward glance. "Yes, I do. Some of these people have been with us for years and have been loyal. I can't allow them to lose their livelihood."

"That's admirable."

Fallon snorted. "I know you think because of how I was raised I don't have a grasp on the plight of the everyday man, but I do, Gage."

She was right. He didn't think she understood, at least not entirely, but she was trying. "I can see that."

"Hey, you two lovebirds," a man wearing a T-shirt with the company logo interrupted. "Would you like to join in? We have a friendly game of tug-of-war going."

Gage turned to Fallon. "You game?"

"Hell, yeah!"

And that's how they spent the afternoon, joined at the hip playing tug-of-war, hunting for treasure and tossing water balloons. The balloons were by far Gage's favorite activity of the day. He hadn't intended it to happen, but when he'd tossed Fallon a balloon, she hadn't caught it. Instead it exploded on her top and revealed her small round breasts to anyone with eyes. He'd immediately grabbed her by the arm and led her to a nearby tent being used as a diaper changing station for small children.

"What's wrong?" Fallon asked when she saw his thunderous expression.

He glanced down at her chest and she followed his eyes to see her nipples protruding through the thin material of her tank top. "Oh!" she exclaimed.

"Yes 'oh,'" he hissed. "Do you have a change of clothes? I can't have you out there looking like that."

She jutted her chin forward and with a smirk asked, "And why not?"

"Those are your employees out there." He pointed behind him. "I don't want the men ogling you."

"You mean, ogling what's yours?"

His eyes narrowed. "That's right, what's mine. Those—" he glanced down at her breasts "—are for my eyes only."

Color washed over her face and neck and Gage could see he'd gotten his point across. "If you were trying to seduce me, you win because," he said, taking a step toward her, "I'm willing to renegotiate our agreement to wait until we're married."

She bit her lip nervously and Gage caught the action. He wanted to soothe her lip with his tongue. But just then she reached inside her pocket and thrust her car keys at him. "I have a bag in the trunk with a change of clothes. Do you mind?"

He shook his head, eager to be out of the fog of desire he was in. "I'll be right back."

Fallon was contemplative after he'd gone. The naked hunger in Gage's eyes frightened her in its intensity because it mirrored her own. They were like two cats in heat, constantly circling one another. They couldn't be alone together. It wasn't a good idea.

Yet she'd enjoyed their day more than she thought she would. Gage was charming and engaging with all her employees. And there was more than one woman who'd given her an envious look throughout the course of the day. Fallon knew how lucky she was. Her eyes had drunk him in when he'd casually strolled to the lemonade stand earlier today. Tall. Good-looking. He looked sexy in his jeans and a T-shirt, with all that leashed testosterone. Fallon had to stop herself from drooling over him.

The games had been a welcome diversion from her riotous emotions and she'd been able to keep her feelings for Gage under wraps. But just now, when his intense dark eyes had landed on her breasts, she'd wanted to rip the damn tank off and beg him to take them in his mouth. That's how much she ached for his touch, for his mouth. Her body still remembered how he'd made her hum in the back seat of the limo.

Heavens. She needed to get a grip. He would be back any moment. He mustn't know the lustful thoughts going through her mind.

Gage returned several minutes later with her bag in tow. "Here you are."

"Thanks." She accepted the bag and rummaged through it, finding the extra tank she'd tossed in. She wanted to put it on, but Gage was staring at her. Awareness was burning in his eyes. "Do you mind turning around so I can put this on?"

"I've already seen it all before," he said, smiling.

"But you still have two more weeks to let the memory sustain you."

His eyes flashed but he spun on his heel, allowing her time to whip the tank over her head. "Damn the two weeks. If you would stop this madness, you and I could do what comes naturally instead of remaining in this constant state of arousal you have me in."

As Fallon adjusted her shirt, Gage's words sank in and she paused. *He was in a constant state of arousal?* It was news to her and she wondered if he'd meant to be so open with his *condition.*

Gage turned around then and caught Fallon in a half state of undress. His gaze met hers and held. Understanding passed between them, as loud and clear as church bells on a Sunday morning. Gage prowled toward her and Fallon sank into his arms. He ran his hands down her body, touching her in all the places she'd been thinking about, dreaming about. He adjusted his stance and shifted her until she was between his thighs and could feel the swell of his arousal at her core. Then he finally gave her what she wanted: his lips on hers.

Their mouths connected. They were hungrily kissing—deeper, harder and longer. Her arms clung tightly around his neck as she held his head in place, their lips meeting in a passion so strong it obliterated everything else. The world ceased to exist and their tongues tangoed and dueled for supremacy. They were both so caught up in the moment they didn't notice they had company until a very loud cough came from behind them.

Startled, they pulled apart and Gage stepped in front of her. It was one of her employees holding a baby in her arms. "I—I'm sorry. I didn't mean to interrupt. I needed to use the tent."

"Of course." Gage spoke up first. "Give us a moment, would you?"

The mother nodded and quickly hurried out.

"That was a close call," Gage said.

"Yeah." Fallon lowered her lashes. "We should go." She started for the exit but Gage stopped her.

"When we're finally together with no interruptions, it's going to be amazing."

And that's what Fallon was afraid of. Because she was starting to fall for Gage Campbell.

Nine

"When are you finally going to get excited about this wedding?" Nora Stewart asked her daughter as the limousine drove them to the bridal gown shop. "You do realize it's only a couple of weeks away? I can't believe you've pushed back getting a dress this long. You're going to have very little time for alterations. Thank God Gage said money was no object because it's going to cost a fortune to turn it around this fast."

"I know, Mother," Fallon said, clenching her teeth. The woman had been on a tirade since the moment they'd gotten in the vehicle, talking about flowers and centerpieces and the like. Fallon didn't care. It didn't mean anything because she wasn't marrying for love. This was an expedient marriage, a marriage of convenience. It wasn't some grand love story.

"Then act like it," her mother responded. "When we go into the bridal shop, you'd better act like the giddy bride. I won't have you embarrassing me with your somber mood."

"Duly noted." Fallon stared out the window. Heaven forbid she embarrass her mother in front of Austin's society ladies. She knew that's why Nora had chosen this particular store. It's where *everyone* went when they wanted a one-of-a-kind, jaw-dropping dress. And she was sure Nora wanted the same for her daughter.

When they arrived, they were immediately greeted by a sophisticated saleswoman. The blonde looked every bit the fashionista in a crepe sheath and Manolo Blahniks. She ushered them to a private area complete with a three-way mirror, pedestal and plush sofa. A bottle of Dom Pérignon was already chilling in a bucket nearby.

As her maid of honor, Shana was already waiting for them on the sofa. "Hey, cuz." She rushed over to give Fallon a hug and then glanced at Nora. "Auntie." Shana's new look consisted of kinky twists that hit her shoulders, a cold-shoulder top and ripped jeans. Fallon was sure her mother was horrified at her niece's appearance.

"Shana." Her mother was not a fan of Fallon's opinionated cousin and had no qualms about showing it. She left them to speak with the staff, allowing Shana to pull Fallon in for a private word.

"How are you doing, cuz?"

"I'm fine."

Shana stared at her. "Are you sure? You're marry-

ing a man you hardly know. And you've allowed your
mother to hijack the whole wedding like it's her own."

"It's fine," Fallon replied. "I told Nora she could
plan to her heart's content."

"Because the wedding means nothing to you?"
Shana asked. "It might not in theory, but it is legal
and binding."

"I'm aware of that, Shana."

"I don't know if you are." Shana shook her head. "I
think you're in way over your head on this one, Fallon.
When I mentioned Gage to you, I thought you'd get a
loan from him. Not go off and marry him."

Fallon shrugged. "What can I say? I like to live
dangerously."

"Yeah, you must. Because Gage Campbell is dangerous to your well-being."

Fallon sighed. "You realize you sound ridiculous,
Shana. Gage would never hurt me."

Shana folded her arms across her chest. "Maybe not
physically, but he could emotionally. I know the huge
crush you carried for this dude. Remember, I listened
to you wax poetic about this man for years. And you're
not like me, moving from man to man. Once you guys
have sex, it's going to be a game changer."

"I may not have your vast experience, but I am capable of guarding my heart."

"You'd better be."

The saleswoman came over and interrupted their
conversation. "Are you ready to find the dress of your
dreams?"

Fallon feigned a smile. "Absolutely."

An hour later Fallon stood on the pedestal staring at herself in the three-way mirror. The wedding dress was everything she never thought she wanted. A shimmering tulle bodice accented in intricate beaded patterns trailed into a voluminous glitter tulle ball gown. Then there were the beaded spaghetti straps gliding from the sweetheart neckline to a sexy V-back with its crystal buttons.

The salesperson added another touch—illusion open-shoulder sleeves accented in beaded lace motifs—and the look was complete. Fallon was a princess.

"She's stunning," her mother cried from the sofa. "This is the one."

Nora had had Fallon try on nearly a dozen dresses before the beleaguered saleswoman had brought out this confection. Nora was right. This was *the one*.

"For once, I'm going to have to agree with Auntie," Shana said. "You've found your dress, Fallon. You look beautiful."

Fallon smiled genuinely for the first time all day. The wedding hadn't seemed real until this very moment. Until she was standing in this fairy-tale gown.

"Are you saying yes to the dress?" the saleswoman asked.

Tears sprung to her eyes and all Fallon could do was nod. She was just so overwhelmed and remained that way during the ride home as she tuned out her mother's nonstop chatter about how the dress would look lovely with the flowers she'd chosen. She was getting married. To Gage. Suddenly, Fallon wanted out of the limo as quickly as humanly possible. She was thankful when her mother exited after a quick kiss on her cheek.

Once she made it to her cottage, she went to her bedroom and fell across the bed. It was happening. She was going to be a wife. Gage's wife. His *lover.*

The implications were finally hitting home when her cell rang. It was Gage, as if he had ESP.

"Hello?" she answered.

"Hey, how'd it go today? Did you find a dress?"

"Yes."

He chuckled. "Are you not going to give me any more than that? No hint? Nothing?"

"I'm sorry. You're going to have to wait until the wedding day."

"Thank God that's only two weeks away. This is the longest month of my life. All the anticipation is driving me crazy."

Fallon sat upright. "Really?"

"Isn't it for you? Aren't you tired of waiting? Don't you want to know if we'll live up to the hype?"

"From what I've experienced thus far, I imagine you're a very good lover," Fallon responded, priding herself on keeping her cool as they discussed their soon-to-be sex life with such casualness.

"I wasn't looking for a compliment," Gage murmured.

"Of course not." Fallon was sure he was very confident in his sexual prowess.

"But I would be lying if I said I wasn't looking forward to the day when you're my wife in every sense of the word."

When they ended the call, Fallon realized she was thinking the exact same thing.

The day of their wedding came much quicker than Fallon would have liked. It seemed as if she'd been trying on dresses with her mother and Shana only yesterday. But the day was finally here and she was a nervous wreck.

She woke up that morning in the Fairmont—where the wedding was being held—with a knot in the pit of her stomach. *Was she doing the right thing?* Logically, she knew that she'd done what she'd had to. Stewart Technologies and its employees depended on her making the right decision. Yet intuitively she knew today would change everything.

"Good morning." Her mother flitted into the room with a tray. "I've come bearing gifts." She approached Fallon and put the tray on the bed. "I have some tea and toast for you. Don't want you to bloat. And some cucumber slices for your eyes." She glanced at Fallon. "You did get some rest last night?"

Fallon nodded but she was lying. It had been hard to sleep. She'd been on pins and needles during the rehearsal dinner, afraid of some sort of outburst. How could she not be? Gage's mother had had to face her parents, the people who'd fired her and run her off the estate. Grace couldn't be happy her son was marrying the daughter of the man she surely despised. It was awkward to say the least.

Nonetheless, Nora acted as if it was water under the bridge and carried on as lady of the manor as she al-

ways did on such occasions. And if Fallon had wanted
to confide in her cousin, that had been impossible because Shana had kept a steady drink in her hand all
night while flirting with Theo, Gage's best man.

As for her fiancé, Gage had been surprisingly stal-
wart all evening. He'd kept his hands to himself the
entire night and only showed signs of affection when
he thought someone was watching. He wasn't his usual
amorous self and it didn't help her mood. When the
night finally ended, Gage had walked her to her suite
and placed a quick peck on her forehead before leaving.

Was he regretting asking her to marry him?

Was that why she was having second thoughts this
morning?

Fallon attempted to eat the toast, but it tasted dry in
her mouth so she sipped on some tea while she slipped
into her robe. One of Austin's top hair stylists and
makeup artists would be here within the hour to begin
working on Shana's, Nora's and Fallon's makeup for
the big day. She wouldn't have much time to herself
after that.

A knock sounded on the door and Shana walked in
wearing sunglasses. "Rough morning?" Fallon asked.

"Yeah, you could say that," Shana murmured, snatch-
ing off her glasses. "How are you doing?"

"I'm fine." Fallon turned her back so her cousin
couldn't read her true emotions. She busied herself
with pulling out the new lingerie she'd purchased for
the day. She was sure Gage would appreciate the silky,
lacy pieces of fabric when he unbuttoned her.

"Fallon, are you sure?" Shana asked, touching her

shoulder. "You don't have to do this. There's still time to change your mind."

"It's normal to have second thoughts," her mother interjected, apparently having overheard their conversation. "I had them when I married your father, but ultimately I knew I was making the right decision. And you are, too, Fallon. You're going to have an amazing life. With a husband as successful as Gage, anything you want will be at your fingertips."

"I thought you didn't like him," Fallon responded evenly.

Her mother chuckled. "I admit he isn't the man I would have chosen for you. But surprisingly he's done quite well for himself, so I have no reservations. Though I doubt Grace agrees. Did you see the evil eye she gave me last night? It was positively wretched."

Of course Nora would take Fallon's wedding day anxiety and make it about her. "Thank you, Mother. Now, if you'll excuse me, I'm going to shower before the dream team arrives."

Fallon quickly rushed off before Shana could say more. Too many thoughts were whirling through her head and she needed some breathing room.

"Are you sure you want to marry her, son?" Grace Campbell asked as she fixed Gage's tie and straightened the lapels of his custom-made tuxedo.

He was surprised she'd come. He thought she'd boycott the ceremony altogether, but she was here supporting him, so he tried to be gentle in his response.

"We've already discussed this, Mother. I have my reasons." *Did she notice he hadn't said love?*

She eyed him warily. "I don't know, Gage. I feel like you're not being truthful with me and there's more to this story. I mean, you tell me you're getting married to the woman who caused us so much misery?"

"She was sixteen when it happened, Mama."

"True, but old enough to know right from wrong, Gage. And she willfully lied about you and cost me my job. Have you honestly forgotten how hard it was for us back then?"

"Of course not."

"Then how can you do this?" She folded her arms across her chest, waiting for his answer.

"Trust me, okay, Mama?" He unfolded her arms and grasped her small hands in his. They weren't as pitiful and worn with cracks and calluses as they'd once been. When he'd made his first million, he'd made sure his mother never had to work another day in her life. "I know what I'm doing."

"I hope you do. Because if this is about revenge, it won't change the past. We have to make our peace with it. And apparently I have to make mine today as I make nice with the Stewarts and watch my only son marry their daughter."

"I don't know if I will ever be at peace after how you and I were both treated, but I've put some measures in place that will settle the score between our families." Theo walked in, breaking up their mother-son moment. "A word, Gage."

Gage nodded. "Be right back, Mama." He left her

in the suite and closed the door behind him because he didn't like the look on Theo's face. "What's wrong?"

"I ran into Shana in the corridor."

"And?"

"She mentioned Fallon was having second thoughts."

"Second thoughts?" Anger blazed through him. "On our wedding day? Fallon had weeks to change her mind. Does she honestly think she can humiliate me and leave me standing at the altar? Where is she?"

"Gage." Theo placed a sobering hand on his arm. "Maybe it's best if you take a minute to cool down."

Gage shrugged his hand off. "Like hell I will. I will not be made a fool of again."

"I'm told she's still in her suite."

Gage wasted no time storming toward the elevator bank. He and Fallon were staying on separate floors to prevent him from seeing her before the ceremony. But he couldn't care less about some stupid superstition. He was acting now. He jabbed the elevator button for the top floor and waited.

His nostrils flared when he thought about Fallon backing out. He simply wouldn't have it. She *would* marry him. He would not have his plans thwarted, not when he was so close.

The elevator arrived and he jumped in. Within minutes, he was knocking on her door. Shana answered and he must have looked thunderous because she immediately backed away. "Where is she?" Gage bellowed.

Shana pointed to the bedroom.

He stalked to the master bedroom and found Fallon seated in front of the mirror with several women surrounding her. She must have heard his voice because she turned and looked behind her. Her face blanched when she saw him.

"It's not good luck for you to see the bride," one of the women objected. But he didn't see them. His focus was on Fallon.

"Leave us," he ordered.

The women glanced at Fallon and she nodded her acquiescence, so they left the room, closing the door behind them.

Damn it. She was stunning with her hair in a mass of pinned-up honey-blond curls. And her face? Well, that was a work of art. Whoever those women were, they knew how to accentuate her best features—her high cheekbones, hazel-gray eyes and pouty lips.

"Are you having second thoughts?" he asked, his eyes never leaving her face. He was afraid to move closer because he feared he'd toss her on the bed and strip her naked and make her agree to be his.

She stared at him for several beats and he wondered if she was going to be stubborn and not answer him. "Yes," she finally replied.

"Then perhaps this will make you reconsider." He pulled out the check he was giving her to save Stewart Technologies and handed it to her.

Fallon stared down at the figure. "I—I thought you weren't giving this to me until we were married."

"I'm not. I'm showing you I've kept up my end of the bargain. In my hands I have the means to save your company from ruin. Are you honestly going to turn your back on the men and women at the barbecue who depend on you, all because you're afraid to be my wife, my lover? You told me you cared about them and their well-being."

Fire flashed in her eyes. "That's not fair. I do care."

"Then prove it. Marry me."

Fallon turned and faced the mirror. He approached to stand right behind her where he could see her reaction. Her eyes were cloudy and he couldn't read her expression. "Fallon, you have a choice. You've always had a choice. Save your company. Or not. The decision is yours."

He turned on his heel and started for the door but she called out after him. "What are you going to do?"

Gage didn't turn around. "I'm going to walk down that aisle as I expect you to." He glanced at his watch. "In an hour."

Gage left the suite. Once he was outside, he leaned against the wall. He didn't know what he was more afraid of. That Fallon wouldn't walk down the aisle. Or that she would.

Ten

"Are you okay?" Fallon heard Shana's voice from behind her. Her hands were shaking so badly she had to clasp them together. She nodded quickly and then felt her cousin's arms wrap around her shoulders. "What did he say?"

"Nothing I didn't already know." She knew what she had to do, but it didn't make it easy. To survive marrying Gage, she'd have to bury her feelings so deep he wouldn't be able to use them against her. She took a deep breath. "Will you help me get into my dress, please?" She spun around and faced Shana.

The look of pity on Shana's face was nearly her undoing but she kept it together. "Yes, I will. If that's what you want."

"I do." Fallon moved toward the elegant princess

dress hanging in the closet and pulled it off the hanger. "It's time."

Fallon didn't remember much else after that. Not removing her robe. Not Shana buttoning her into the delicate beaded fabric of her dress. Not her mother bursting in with the flowers, handing Fallon her bouquet and helping put on her veil. The next thing Fallon knew, she was in the elevator with Shana, her mother and the wedding planner, who held her train.

It was only when she was walking down the corridor and saw her father standing resplendent in a formal white tuxedo that she snapped out of it. He slid his arm through hers and looked down at her. "You've never looked lovelier, baby girl. Are you ready to do this?"

She nodded. And slowly the doors to the ballroom opened and they were walking down the aisle.

Fallon saw Gage standing at the end, waiting for her. He looked sinfully handsome, just as he had earlier when he'd walked into her bedroom and taken her breath away. He hadn't needed to show her the check. Although she'd had doubts earlier, she'd gotten through them and had already planned to marry him. But seeing how upset Gage was that she might back out showed her this marriage meant something to him whether he was willing to admit it or not.

Or at least that's the lie she fed herself as she made her way up the aisle to him. When she arrived at the altar, her father placed her hand in Gage's and her breath caught in her throat. He rewarded her with a smile, which she returned.

She could do this. Would do this. Why? Because Gage meant more to her than she was willing to admit.

Gage had never been happier than when he saw Fallon walking down in the aisle in that magnificent dress. He was glad he hadn't seen her wearing it earlier and they could retain some tradition because, quite literally, she was breathtaking. He found himself having to truly listen to the minister's words to be able to repeat the traditional vows to love, protect, honor and cherish her.

He sensed Fallon was nervous because her hands were shaking as he placed the ring on her finger and she did the same to him. But she didn't back out. She honored her commitment to him and when they were pronounced husband and wife, Gage was beyond ecstatic. He slid his arm around her petite waist and pulled her to him. Then he softly kissed her before pulling away. They'd have all the time in the world later in the presidential suite when he would finally make Fallon his.

The reception was a blur. There were handshakes and hugs from friends, acquaintances and employees who were there to celebrate their wedding. There were frowns from Fallon's parents and Ayden, who were both there on sufferance. Ayden had only stayed for the wedding and stood in the shadows while her younger brother, Dane, chose to not attend at all. He only remembered the moments when it was the two of them.

Nora had transformed the ballroom into a winter fairyland. Crystal chandeliers hung from the ceilings, illuminating an explosion of beautiful white flowers.

Frosted trees, sparkling crystal garlands and candles were everywhere. Nora had decorated each table in white and silver while their sweetheart table had two thronelike chairs.

For their first dance Gage held Fallon in his arms and she felt so good, but delicate in a way he couldn't quite put his finger on. Then there was the cake cutting. Rather than use a fork, he'd used his fingers to feed Fallon a piece. She'd been shocked at first, but had opened her mouth and accepted it, wiping his fingers clean with her tongue. It had been the most singularly erotic moment of his life.

He was thankful when the night began winding down. He made quite the show of going underneath Fallon's dress to get her garter, which Theo caught while her cousin Shana caught Fallon's bouquet. Gage sure hoped there wasn't a love connection there. He doubted Theo could handle Shana; she was a whole lot of woman.

Finally the night was over and he and Fallon were able to escape the ballroom to head upstairs as they were sent off with bubbles and well-wishes. They were led to an elevator exclusively for their getaway. Gage took her hand but it was a bit cold and clammy.

"Are you all right?"

"Yes."

"You haven't given me much tonight, Fallon," Gage said. "You've been quiet. Reserved, even."

"I kept up my end of the bargain, yes?" She turned away from him and Gage didn't like it.

"About earlier—"

"You made your point," Fallon interrupted, looking straight ahead. "And I heard you, okay? The day was a bit...overwhelming."

He squeezed her hand and she finally glanced in his direction. "It was for me, as well. I'm sorry, too, if I came across a bit..." He searched for the right word. "Rough. I always seem to be that way with you. Can we agree to put it behind us?" He needed things between them to be okay, because he was so ready to start their life together *in bed*.

She gave a hesitant smile. "Yes."

The presidential suite was a honeymooner's paradise complete with chocolate-covered strawberries, a bucket of champagne chilling in the living room and a trail of red rose petals leading to the master bedroom. Dozens of candles gave the room a romantic glow. Fallon stared at the enormous bed, picked up her train and came back into the living room. She wasn't ready to face the night ahead.

Once Fallon entered the room, Gage held up the bottle. "Care for champagne?"

"I'd love some." Fallon needed liquid courage for what was ahead. She didn't know how not to show her true feelings because her heart was involved now. Her whole heart. Somehow she'd tripped into a state of love without knowing it and she knew with certainty Gage could break her heart. Because for Gage tonight was all about desire. Sexual desire. And she felt it, too. This raw, carnal, all-consuming lust. It was why she was so out of control whenever they were together. Even now her stomach was pulled tight in knots wondering what it would be like to *be* with him.

Gage made Fallon aware of her own body and she knew before the night was over he would become familiar with every inch of it. Of that she was sure. It was in the flare of his eyes as they drifted over her. He handed her a flute of champagne. She accepted and downed the entire glass in one gulp.

"There's no need to be nervous, Fallon," Gage assured her as he sat on the couch. "We have all night. There's no rush. Come here." He patted the seat next to him.

At first Fallon didn't move a muscle but when he gave her an imploring look, she relented and sat. "This feels a little surreal."

Gage reached for her hand and turned it over. When he did, the impressive six-carat diamond ring he'd purchased caught the light. He fingered it with his thumb. "I would disagree. It feels very real."

He cupped her face in one hand. "Is it really so scary to be married to me, Fallon?" His thumb swept across her lips, making her flesh tingle.

"I'm not scared," Fallon responded. "I made a choice and I stand behind it."

Gage straightened. "I'm glad. I would hate for you to regret the time we spend together."

Fallon had her doubts about the marriage but not about the pleasure she would find in Gage's arms. Leaning forward, his lips found hers. It wasn't a tentative kiss, nor was it a kiss meant to entice. The touch of his mouth was soft, yet it shot volts of electricity right through Fallon and she wanted more. When he lowered his head again it wasn't to her closed mouth—she'd already parted her lips. She gave in to his hungry mouth. Her hands moved to his chest and upward to link her arms around his neck to bring him closer, but Gage pulled away.

She didn't understand. "What's wrong?"

"I promised you we'd take this slow…"

Fallon rose and held out her hand. "I don't want it slow."

His dark eyes landed on hers and Fallon's breath caught in her throat. Slowly and seductively his gaze traveled over her face, searching her eyes. For doubt? He wouldn't find any. They were married and it was time. Gage must have seen her acceptance because he was on his feet within seconds and they were walking to the bedroom.

They stopped at the foot of the bed. Fallon felt Gage's hands on the back of her dress as he unbuttoned each crystal button until eventually she felt a cold gust of air against her back. Then Gage's fingers were on her shoulders, easing down the sheer gossamer straps until the dress fell to her waist.

She felt his mouth pressing soft kisses on her shoulder and tried to steady herself, but a dizzying current of attraction raced through her as he wet her neck with his tongue. He used his fingers to caress, tease and stroke her bare breasts. There hadn't been a need for a bra because it came built-in. She was naked and completely open to Gage, her husband. His palms cupped her aching breasts and when he skated his thumbs across her engorged nipples, she let out a low moan.

"You're so sensitive," he rasped and continued brushing his thumbs over her breasts. Fallon closed her eyes, allowing her head to fall back against the wall of his chest. Gage held her to him, pressing her hard against him and leaned down, rewarding her with a deep kiss, which merely increased their mounting desire. She spun around to face him.

"Tell me what you want," Gage rasped.

"I want you." To prove it she stepped out of the flowing dress, letting it pool at her feet until she was standing in nothing but her thong and bejeweled high heels.

"God, you're beautiful!" Before she could react, he sank to his knees in front of her and moved his hands to her hips until he arrived at her inner thighs.

"What are you doing?"

"Tasting you." He slid his finger along the edge of her lace thong and Fallon hissed out a breath. He pushed the fabric aside and his thumb traced along her cleft. Fallon jerked when his fingers delved and began gently exploring her inner folds. He lifted his head to look at her and smiled. "Hot *and* wet."

She was consumed with heat and when he slid one finger inside her, she shuddered. "Oh." But there was more to come, because he slowly withdrew it, only to add another finger. Meanwhile his thumb was working her clitoris. Pleasure was building, taking her to a fever pitch, making her want to whisper his name like some sort of mantra. "Gage, please—"

He wasn't listening, he merely plunged his fingers deeper inside her, filling her. "You like that?"

"Yes," she implored when he repeated the action, "but I—I need more."

"Like what?"

"Your mouth. I need your mouth on me." Fallon was embarrassed to say it out loud. She'd never been so vocal with her desires, but if she couldn't tell her husband, who could she tell?

Gage gripped her hips and within seconds had deposited her on the bed and disposed of her thong. Fallon shamelessly spread her legs and watched as he cupped her bottom and then raked her with his tongue. She arched off the bed, but Gage held her firm. His hands were against her pelvis, spreading her legs wide so his tongue could work her over and over again with such sensuous abandon that Fallon squirmed, begging him to end it.

He merely laughed and continued flicking his tongue over her core, laving her with deliberate yet feather-light movements. He had her wound so tight, she was aching for him to relieve the pressure building inside her. And when he circled her clitoris with his tongue while simultaneously pumping his fingers deep inside her, a scream rang out from deep within her.

"Omigod!" Fallon pressed her hands to her face, but Gage refused to allow her to hide.

Instead he crawled up her body and gave her an openmouthed kiss. It was heady and erotic because she could taste herself on his lips.

"Don't hide. I want to see your face. I want to know you're enjoying our lovemaking."

Eventually, when her breathing returned, she smiled. "Don't you think you're wearing too many clothes?" She was naked while he was fully clothed save for the jacket and tie he'd discarded when they'd walked in.

"Indeed, I am, Mrs. Campbell. Care to help me with that?"

Gage sat upright and watched Fallon as she excitedly attacked the buttons on his shirt. When they didn't unbutton fast enough, she ripped it open and buttons went flying. He liked that she was as desperate and eager as he was for their union. The anticipation was heightened by the fact they'd waited a month—hell, years—to get here and he supposed that's why it felt so momentous. He was making love to his *wife*.

Fallon was his. There was no escaping it. She'd signed her name on the marriage certificate, sealing her fate. Because tonight he intended to possess her. Over and over again until they were both spent.

As she pulled the shirt down his shoulders and he shrugged it off his arms, Gage felt like a king. He moved off the bed long enough to strip off his pants and boxers and then, naked, he joined her on the bed. He reached for one of her feet that were still encased in her bejeweled shoes. "These are incredible," he said with a grin as he unbuckled the ankle straps.

"And they cost a fortune," Fallon responded as he removed one and then the other. He took the pins out from the elaborate updo and ran his fingers through the mass of honey-blond hair.

Finally he could feast his eyes on her with no barriers. And he certainly looked his fill, from her round breasts to her slim waist to her flat stomach to the curve of her hips, before ending his tour with the patch of dark curls between her thighs. He wanted to reach out and touch her, but Fallon took over. She pushed him back against the pillows and straddled him. Her silky-soft hair slid onto his chest as their mouths fused together, tongues tangling in heated lust. Gage dragged his head back; he wanted to look at her. Her eyes were wide and dilated while her lips were parted and swollen. His need for her grew exponentially and he reached for her again, this time putting his mouth on one of her full, round breasts. His tongue swirled around her nipple, which tightened and puckered. She threw back her head in abandon so he took his time worshipping the bud and then paid homage to its twin with his mouth and tongue.

"Hmm...no fair," she murmured when he finally lifted his head. "I'm on top. I'm supposed to be in charge."

"Oh, but you are," Gage said as his fingers moved between them to slip through her slick folds. He dipped inside and found her as wet as when he'd made her come earlier. It was time. He was throbbing with a need to be inside her and now there was no need for protection. Last week, Fallon had asked whether he'd been tested. It was a fair question given they were becoming lovers and he'd answered honestly that he was clean. She'd shared the same news and they'd agreed she would be on the pill. Gage was happy because there would be no barriers between them. Just two people sharing the most sensuous of acts.

He grasped her hips and lifted her so the wide tip of his erection nudged at the entrance to her hot, damp flesh. She gasped, but he held her firm as she took him deep inside her. He loved the way her tight core clenched around his thick, hard, pulsating length, but he wanted more. He thrust his hips upward in one savage thrust and impaled her.

"Oh, God!" Fallon moaned, resting her palms on his chest. Her eyes were closed and he couldn't read her expression no matter how badly he wanted to.

"Look at me, baby," Gage urged and, when she did, he caught the passion in those hazel-gray depths and knew this was more than sex.

Fallon moved, lifting off him and then coming back down again. Over and over. She eased off and down onto him. Gage was blind with lust, gripping her hips and urging her on, but Fallon was in control, undulating against him, finding her own rhythm. He met her by pumping his hips up as his entire body stirred to life. He reached for her, his tongue raking her lips, demanding entry, and she parted for him. Gage thrust deep inside her mouth, mimicking the movements of their lower bodies. He heard Fallon's breath hitch and could feel her body tensing as if she was poised on the abyss. He wanted them to go over the cliff together so his thrusts became deeper, harder and more animalistic in nature.

Fallon moaned when he cupped her buttocks, so he drove harder until soon her body was clenching around him and pushing them both over the edge as he found his release.

Gage growled as the world righted itself and Fallon quivered over him, slumping against him. He'd suspected but hadn't been prepared for how sexually compatible they were. He was already feeling a resurgence of desire after being completely satisfied moments ago. The voracious hunger he had for her couldn't last, right? Because if it did, it would derail all of his best laid plans.

Eleven

Fallon woke with a start. Sunshine was streaming through the sheer curtains.

She'd succumbed to every illicit sensation Gage evoked throughout the course of the night. She wanted everything he had to offer. Gage understood and matched her in his unparalleled desire. Not once, not twice, but three times last night, their coupling had been wild and erotic. At one point he'd lifted her legs to his shoulders and she'd arched into him as he'd pumped into her, hard and fast, until she'd panted out his name.

Fallon hadn't known sex could be that good, that she could literally burn up with wanting for a man. But it was what Gage brought out in her. And that scared her because although it was thrilling, Fallon knew loving Gage was dangerous. They were in a temporary marriage of convenience, one that allowed them to both get what they wanted, though Fallon still didn't understand what she'd brought to the table. Status? Acceptance into Austin society? She would have given up her status in a heartbeat to have Gage fall in love with her.

Her husband stirred beside her. "Good morning," he slurred with eyes half open. "What are you doing up? Did I not wear you out last night?" When she didn't respond right away, he continued. "Then I didn't fulfill my husbandly duties."

Gage rolled over, positioning himself above her. "Gage…" she sighed as molten heat formed in her core.

"Hmm…don't worry. I'll be gentle." Slowly he nudged her entrance with his shaft, all the while looking straight at her. There was no hiding behind a façade. Fallon had no choice but to stare into his intense eyes as he thrust deep inside her.

There was a fierce need for possession in his eyes and Fallon was surprised by the depth of emotion she saw there. *Did Gage care for her more than she thought?* Fallon couldn't say because he gave her no reprieve. Instead he continued his merciless assault, molding her closer, pressing their bodies together so he could go deeper. Take her higher. Urgency expanded within her until Fallon's entire body erupted and she saw stars.

She struggled not to give away too much with her expression, but Gage surged inside her again and again and the delicious friction of their bodies caused her to come apart. She clutched at his biceps as another orgasm overtook her. Gage groaned in her ear and she tasted his passion as his tongue pressed past her lips to caress and stroke hers.

When he collapsed on top of her, his breathing slowly began to even out. Then he shifted to his side and relieved her of his weight. Fallon stroked his cheek and traced his mouth with her fingers. The uncontrollable lust and hunger for Gage was like nothing she'd ever known. This man was burrowing into her soul.

"Are you all right?" he asked, searching her face.

"Yes."

He touched the bridge of her nose. "But you're pensive. I can see the thoughts whirling around in your brain. Let them go, Fallon, and be present in the moment with me."

"I am."

"You're thinking about later and what comes next. About why it's so good between us. Isn't it enough that it is? Can't we enjoy each other?"

Until it peters out, Fallon wanted to add but didn't. She nodded.

"Good." Gage smiled.

Gage stared at Fallon from his poolside seat at the luxury resort in Punta Cana where they were staying for their honeymoon. He couldn't resist watching her every move as she made her way to him. His wife was a knockout. She wore a halter-style bikini held together by rings in the center of her bust and along the sides of her slim hips. It did wonders for her cleavage. Her round, pert breasts were pushed up and enhanced for the entire world to see. Although she'd wrapped a sarong around her waist, Gage knew men were looking.

The last several days they'd been soaking in the sun and swimming in the private pool of their beachside villa. Fallon had teased him he was keeping her naked and barefoot. They'd hardly left the villa except for a romantic candlelit dinner he'd arranged on the beach upon their arrival and the one day they'd spent sightseeing and snorkeling. Today they'd finally ventured out to the main building and now Gage wished they were in their private world again. He didn't like men wanting what was his. Because Fallon was *his.*

They'd been together in every possible position. He was very imaginative and Fallon had been enthusiastic about all of his ideas, adding a few of her own that had him begging and pleading with her for more. Her soft cries of delight, her hungry moans as their bodies moved faster and came together in mind-blowing release, were overwhelming. When it came to his wife, Gage was insatiable. But it was more than that. He'd thought that once they became intimate, his ache for her would go away. Instead it seemed to have metastasized and he was incapable of controlling himself. He wanted her all the time, but their marriage had an expiration date.

At least that was the verbal agreement they had. At the time, Gage hadn't seen a problem. He assumed he'd be ready to move on when the hunger and passion subsided. Plus, he had a plan in place to take over Stewart Technologies once he had enough stock. He'd already purchased a substantial amount on the open market with his holding companies. Now it was a matter of finding those investors who were eager to sell.

Gage tried not to think about how this would affect Fallon. He couldn't. Business was business. What they shared was something altogether different. Something that was just between them. Special, even.

"I arranged for our massages on the beach," Fallon said as they retreated to the loungers in their private cabana.

"Sounds marvelous." Gage eyed her as she removed the sarong from around her slim waist to reveal the barely there bikini that covered her curvy bottom and the patch of curls between her thighs. Thinking about when he'd been buried there this morning had his penis stiffening in his swim shorts.

Fallon reached for her drink, a fruity concoction inside a pineapple. He'd opted for a beer. "I had to do something. Otherwise, we'd never enjoy any of the resort's luxurious amenities."

"I have all I want right here." His eyes scanned hers. She blushed as she always did when he talked about their lovemaking. Over the course of the last four days, he'd made it his mission in life to help her shed her inhibitions. They'd made love in the shower, pool, hot tub, even on the beach near their villa. That had taken a little more coaxing, but once his hands and mouth had been on her, Fallon had given in and allowed him to have his way with her.

He smiled at the memory.

"What's so funny?" she inquired.

"Just remembering the other night on the beach."

Fallon's face flamed.

"And hoping for a repeat."

"You're terrible, Gage. And that's not going to happen. We could have been caught. If anyone had found us, I would have been so embarrassed."

"Trust me, babe. We weren't the only ones out there," he replied. "This is an adults-only resort, known for honeymooners and anniversaries."

Fallon shrugged, placed her pineapple on the table between the loungers and eased back. "We'll leave them to their shenanigans. I prefer the privacy of our villa."

"And where's the fun in that?"

Their butler, James, came to the cabana, interrupting the moment. "Mr. and Mrs. Campbell, can I get you anything? Another refreshment, perhaps?" He nodded to their drinks on the table. "Or a light snack?"

"I would love some fresh fruit," Fallon said. "And maybe some cheese and crackers?"

"Another beer for me," Gage answered.

Once James departed, Gage turned to Fallon. "I have a very special evening planned for our last night here."

"I can't believe the honeymoon is nearly over. Why did we only give ourselves five days?"

"Because someone—" he glanced in her direction "—is a workaholic and refused to take the entire week. But don't you worry, I will make tonight unforgettable."

Gage made certain the evening was beyond Fallon's wildest imagination. After their afternoon massages, they'd gone back to the room where her husband had turned showering into an erotic experience. He'd thoroughly soaped and washed her body with his hands before falling to the floor in the oversize super shower and loving her with his mouth. Then he'd hoisted her off her feet and made passionate love to her against the tiled wall while water pounded on his back. Fallon had melted into a sea of lust as she did whenever she was around him. His every touch, kiss and possession caused an inferno of passion to consume her.

Eventually they'd left their villa and ended up on a yacht for a sunset cruise Gage had arranged. It took them around the island while they enjoyed a four-course meal prepared by a private chef in the state-of-the-art kitchen belowdecks. The captain had given them a tour of the yacht's modern amenities when they'd come aboard; it had a kitchen, living area, dining room, two guest bedrooms and a master suite complete with a king-size bed and full-size master bathroom.

Now they were on the deck, lying on the plush recliners and stargazing while drinking Cristal. Fallon had chosen to wear a simple color-blocked maxi dress in deep orange, navy and white, pairing it with low-heeled white sandals. It was nautical and comfortable. Gage had opted for linen trousers and some sort of tunic shirt he'd picked up during their one and only sightseeing trip. But all she could see when she closed her eyes were those broad shoulders, chiseled eight-pack abs and trim waist.

Fallon felt fulfilled in Gage's arms. For the first time in her life, she was beginning to understand the addiction to sex. It hadn't even been a week and she wanted Gage with a pride-destroying hunger. She, who had never *needed* anyone, needed him.

Which was why Fallon was looking forward to flying home tomorrow. Life would go back to normal after the craziness of the wedding and honeymoon. She would dive back into work immediately. She had some thoughts on paring down the staff by retiring some of her father's old friends and bringing in new talent who were forward thinking.

"Penny for your thoughts?" Gage inquired.

"I'm thinking about going home."

Gage frowned. "I didn't realize spending 24/7 with me was such a chore."

Their eyes met.

"Of course not. I've enjoyed our time together."

"But you're ready to get back to work?" Gage finished.

Fallon shrugged. "There's much to be done to get Stewart Technologies back on track. I'll be very busy."

"Is that your subtle way of telling me that you'll be too busy or too tired to fulfill your wifely duties? Because that's not going to fly."

"No… I—" Fallon wasn't able to utter another word because Gage's long body came up and over hers, crushing her against the lounger as his heavy, muscular legs slid on either side of the thin fabric of her dress, caging her in. Her head fell back as Gage gave her a fierce, demanding kiss, plundering her mouth with his invading tongue. He was like a marauder, taking what he wanted.

She felt the weight of one of his palms at her ankles as he slid the maxi dress up her thigh.

"Gage, wait!" Fallon stopped his hand. "What about the staff?"

"They've all retired for the evening, per my instructions." Then he was underneath the hem, his hands searing every inch of her skin. Instinctively, she pressed herself further into his touch. Their bodies shifted and she was able to feel the hardness of his erection against her core. Fallon was needy and hungry—for him and no one else. His body was like a drug. When he touched her, what little was left of her functioning brain gave way to pure lust and all rational thought fled her body.

He lifted his mouth to trail kisses along her face and jaw, murmuring, "I had better get my fill now."

And so had she.

She feverishly tugged at his shirt. He had too many clothes on. Within seconds, he'd pulled it up and over his head. Electricity buzzed when she felt the crisp brush of his chest hair on her fingertips. She lowered her head and pressed her lips against the wall of his chest, tasting and tantalizing him with no restraint.

"Fallon…"

She liked how his voice was rough and raw with emotion, so she continued her ministrations. But Gage stopped her. Clenching his hands in her hair, he pulled her away so he could crush his mouth against hers in a hungry kiss turned sensual dance. She felt his urgent hands at her waist as he levered himself away long enough to remove the maxi dress and leave her naked save for the thong she'd been wearing. She'd taken to going braless the entire honeymoon.

"I want you so bad," he growled and cupped her breasts, teasing them into aroused peaks with swirls and flicks of his tongue and nips of his teeth.

"Me, too." She clenched her hands around the corded muscles of his biceps. The man had a wicked way with his tongue. She arched against his invasion, all the while feeling the hot moisture of need between her thighs that only he could assuage. She began shoving his trousers and his underwear down his legs. He stood long enough to rid himself of the offending garments before they were back together on the lounger.

"This has to go," he said and gave her thong a gentle tug, snapping the fabric asunder.

That was fine with Fallon; she didn't care about restraint. She wanted him right here, right now—regardless of who might find them. This is what he'd done to her: he'd made her a mass of need. His hands slid between them to brush the damp curls between her thighs. She was already wet and he easily slid not one but two fingers inside her. She encouraged him by moving with his hand. She was so desperate to come, but he didn't let her.

"I want to come with you," he murmured, removing his hands. His legs came between hers, nudging them apart. She spread her legs wider, inviting him in, and he surged inside her in one powerful movement.

Fallon let out a sharp, keening cry of delight and her arms went around his neck as she brought his mouth back down to hers. She was on fire. He pushed in again then withdrew. Fallon wanted to cry out in protest but he surged in further, deeper, than he had before. She wrapped her thighs around him and reveled in the way Gage took her higher, again and again, until there was only them, as connected as two people could be. Fallon arched her hips when he angled himself so he could take her harder and faster. The storm built, swirling until there was nowhere else to go but over the edge. Simultaneously they tumbled into ecstasy and cried out their release.

And Fallon knew, as she'd known for days, that somewhere along the line, passion had developed into love.

Twelve

After realizing the depth of her feelings for her husband in Punta Cana, Fallon hoped returning to Austin would give her peace. It didn't. The time they'd spent together during the honeymoon had been a revelation. Her husband wasn't the arrogant, bossy alpha male she'd thought she knew. Instead he'd been relaxed and easygoing, as if a weight had been lifted off his shoulders. And in bed he'd been a passionate yet tender and giving lover.

She was just as crazy about Gage as she'd been before except now, a month after the honeymoon, she knew even more about the man. It frightened her to know she could be in a love with a man who didn't return her feelings and considered her an added bonus to their business arrangement. Once they'd come back to the States, Gage immediately moved her into his pent-house and ensconced her even deeper into his world. Morning, noon and night, he was either in her head with constant calls or texts to check in to see how her day was going or making surprise visits to her office just to take her to lunch. And the nights…oh, the nights were something else entirely.

If Fallon thought she would get some sort of reprieve from their lovemaking, she'd been wrong. Gage was as hungry for her as he'd been on their honeymoon, maybe even more so. He seemed determined to not let her keep her distance. *Did he know that had been her goal?* On the plane ride home, Fallon had decided to limit sex between them, but Gage had seduced her nearly every night since. It was so intense, she'd had to beg off the other night, claiming it was the wrong time of the month. She knew her excuse wouldn't hold much longer, but the last few days had been bliss. She'd finally been able to clear her head of the sexual fog.

As she drove home late Friday evening, Fallon contemplated how she had to face facts. She was hopelessly in love with Gage. She'd been carrying a torch for him ever since she was a young girl. It had only grown when she'd thrown herself at him and he'd kissed her with such fervor. It was a double-edged sword knowing she was Gage's wife and loved him with heart and soul, but at the same time he didn't love her and had only married her for lust and acceptance into society.

How was she going to navigate the next five months feeling this way? It was going to be pure torture, but somehow she would. She had to turn off her emotions, not give herself completely over to Gage as she'd been doing. She had to focus on self-preservation because their marriage of convenience would end in the near term.

She pulled her Audi into the parking space next to Gage's Bugatti and turned off the engine. She inhaled, mentally steeling herself for the evening ahead, and eased out of the car. The ride to Gage's building had seemed like the longest ride of her life. But when she finally entered their living room, the atmosphere was relaxed. Jazz was playing softly in the background, candles were lit and the smells coming from the kitchen caused her stomach to stir. She'd only had a salad for lunch and that had been hours ago.

Gage came padding toward her barefoot, wearing low-slung jeans and a T-shirt, two wineglasses in his hands. "Thought you might need this after a long day of work." He handed her a glass, which she accepted.

"Thank you." Fallon had always imagined having a marriage like this one day, but she'd never dreamed of Gage in the role of caring husband. She followed him into the living room and plonked down on the sofa. She was about to remove her stilettos when Gage joined her and took over the task, removing one shoe and then the other. He helped her remove the suit jacket she'd worn, revealing the thin cami underneath.

When his gaze zeroed in on her breasts, Fallon felt as if she were naked because on cue her nipples pebbled at his searing gaze. She reached for her wineglass and liberally drank.

"Was it that bad at the office?" Gage asked, watching her intently. "I thought things were settling down a bit."

"They are," Fallon said. "I've settled some debts and made payment arrangements with other creditors. As we discussed last week, I want to use some of those funds for development to make Stewart Technologies what it once was."

"Did you meet with the head of R and D yet?"

Fallon was happy they were talking shop. She'd been nervous because he'd given her one of those hungry gazes when she'd come in, which usually ended up with her on her back. Or on top. Or on the side. Or the floor. It didn't much matter.

"Fallon?"

He was speaking to her. "Oh, yes, I did."

Over the delicious dinner a private chef had made for them, they continued discussing the viability of several options the department head had come up with. Gage opened up about some new deals he was working on and she offered advice Gage seemed to find valuable. Fallon relaxed as the evening progressed, especially when they retired to the sofa and streamed some television shows on Hulu. An hour in, Fallon couldn't help but stifle a yawn.

"Tired?" Gage asked.

She nodded.

"C'mon, let me put you to bed." Gage rose and helped her up.

Once they were in the bedroom, Fallon went about her normal routine of preparing for bed, but she felt Gage's eyes on her every movement. She knew she was pushing it when she reached for a sexy nightie. It had spaghetti straps and stopped midthigh, but it was clothing. Since their honeymoon, she'd forgone pajamas because she and Gage were so insatiable for each other.

After washing her face and brushing her teeth, she headed to her side of the bed. Gage was sitting upright with his phone in hand, but appearances were deceiving. Fallon didn't doubt for a second he hadn't noticed her attire. She slid in beside him, turned off the lamp and faced the opposite direction. She heard him move around before the room fell into darkness. Fallon tried to calm her breathing and act as if she were falling asleep, but Gage called her out.

"I know you're not asleep, Fallon."

"Nearly. I'm exhausted."

She felt his arms encircle her as he pulled her firmly to him until her backside was against his very hard shaft. She sucked in a breath.

"Too tired for this?" He planted hot, openmouthed kisses on her neck until he came to her ear and gently tugged on the lobe with his mouth.

Sweet Jesus! He knew all her erogenous zones. Fallon closed her eyes and willed herself to stay strong. "Not tonight, all right?" Fallon managed to say despite her body's yearnings. "It's been a long day."

"That didn't seem to bother you before. Why now?"

Anger coursed through her and she spun around to face him in the darkness. "Really, Gage, I ask for one night to sleep and suddenly I'm in the wrong? Or am I supposed to be at your beck and call every night? Is that what you expected out of this arrangement? Because if so, you're in for a rude awakening. I'm my own person with my own mind, my own thoughts, my own feelings."

"I recognize that, Fallon. I didn't realize I was pressuring you. I thought the feeling was mutual and you wanted me just as much. Consider me duly warned off." He turned away and this time his back was to her.

Fallon felt terrible. She hadn't meant to hurt him, but she'd needed some breathing room because she was afraid of the tender feelings she'd developed. Afraid he might see them and then where would they be? She had to stay the course. It was best not only for her sanity but her pride.

Gage ran. On Saturday morning, he ran as fast as he could on the treadmill in his building's gym until he'd exhausted himself. He hadn't slept much last night because Fallon had shut him down. Literally. There was no mistaking the off-limits sign she'd been wearing for days, except last night she'd made it very clear she didn't want him. Before she'd been more than happy to sleep nude because they'd been so attuned to each other's needs.

Over the last month they'd awaken during the middle of the night and reach for each other. Sometimes he started it. Sometimes she did. They'd make love into the wee hours of the morning and *now* she was tired. Tired of him? Gage wondered.

He'd seen the way she responded to him. Felt her clench around his shaft when he'd been buried deep inside her. Watched the bliss come over her when she'd climaxed. Why? Because he'd felt it himself. An unexplainable ecstasy had plagued him since they'd become intimate. He'd thought he'd get the hunger for her out of his system, but he hadn't. And he'd tried. Perhaps he'd come on too strong? No. No. No.

He wasn't wrong about how Fallon felt about him. If he was honest, there were times another emotion had been visible in her expression. Something he was afraid to say out loud. She hadn't been able to hide it, but she'd tried to. And now she was acting as if their lovemaking had become burdensome when that was far from the case. She was feeling too much the same as him.

He was on the verge of everything he'd wanted in this marriage. The other day he'd secured another five percent of Stewart Technologies' stock, bringing his total to forty-five percent. He'd been slowly acquiring the stock through several holding companies to ensure it wouldn't be traced back to him. As for his wife, the attraction he'd felt for her had materialized into the most spectacular sex of his life. The problem was, the triumph he'd thought he'd feel as the moment of success got nearer left a bitter taste in his mouth.

Whoever said revenge was a dish best served cold had no idea what it would feel like mixed with white-hot sexual need. The anger he'd felt toward Fallon and her family was the reason he'd chosen to go down this path, but it was getting harder and harder not to want more out of this relationship than either one of them had wanted to give.

Gage stopped running and pressed the stop button on the treadmill.

The marriage was convenient. Fallon got her money and he got Stewart Technologies and Fallon in his bed. However, Gage wasn't satisfied. He wanted both, but deep down he knew there was going to come a time he would have to choose.

Thirteen

"Are you sure you want me to attend this dinner with you two?" Grace asked from the back seat of Gage's car. Gage had invited his mother to come to Thanksgiving at the Stewarts' with Fallon and him, because his wife had adamantly refused to miss it, claiming she always shared the meal with her parents.

"Of course. We want you there." He hazarded a glance at Fallon, but she was staring out the window. When Gage had first invited Grace, he'd been certain she would decline, but he'd been wrong. She claimed she hadn't seen much of him since the wedding and didn't plan on missing out on the holiday.

Gage wasn't looking forward to the hostility that could break out on all sides tonight. He and Fallon hadn't been on good terms in weeks. The night after she'd re-

fused to make love, Gage had felt hurt and so he'd chosen to withhold any affection. The problem was, he was
hurting himself in the process because he missed being
close to his wife, but he was too proud to admit he was
wrong and so their standoff had continued.

"I made one of my famous sweet potato pies," his
mother said. "Wonder if Nora will mind."

"I'm sure Mother will welcome the pie."

She didn't.

When they entered Stewart Manor, the matriarch
had air-kissed his mother and then handed the pie off
to the butler, never to be seen the rest of the evening.
From then on, Nora was overly solicitous, which made
his mother uncomfortable. The night didn't get any
better, especially when Dane called to inform them
he'd missed his flight and wouldn't make it. Meanwhile Henry kept giving Gage the evil eye. And why
wouldn't he? Fallon was being as warm as a lump of
coal. Could her father sense their acrimony?

After dinner they retired to the family room and the
night went further downhill.

"So what have you been up to, Grace?" Nora inquired.

"I wasn't cleaning houses, if that's what you're after.
I've been retired for years because my son takes great
care of me. He even bought me a house in Lost Creek."
She winked at her son.

"You really have done well, Gage." Nora smiled.
"You take care of your mother while our daughter
harps about our spending and has placed us on allow-

ance. Or was that your doing?" She eyed Gage suspiciously.

"No, Mother, it was mine." Fallon perked up after being surly all night. "Perhaps if you learned to curb your spending, I wouldn't be in the position I'm in."

"Married to my son?" Grace inquired. "You would do well to remember he forgave you your past transgressions, my dear."

"Leave my daughter out of this, Grace. Your beef is with me," Fallon's father interjected.

Grace glared at him. "Do you blame me, Henry?" She used his given name, which she never would have years ago. "I'm still waiting on an apology."

"Mama…" Gage didn't need his mother to defend him.

"Don't *Mama* me." Grace stood. "You ask me to make *nice* with these people when they've yet to acknowledge the harm they caused both of us. And now…" Her eyes bore into Fallon, but one look at Gage made her not finish her sentence. "Please take me home."

"That might be best," Nora responded.

"Don't patronize me, Nora Stewart, when you can't be bothered to clean your own house or make your own meals. You would do well to learn a little humility as fortunes change." His mother walked to the exit and Gage made to follow her but looked at Fallon. "Are you coming?"

Fallon shook her head. "I'll stay here, if you don't mind. I'll get a taxi home."

Gage clenched his jaw. He didn't want to get into

a fight in front of the Stewarts. "Fine. I'll see you at home."

On the way back to her house, his mother made it clear that, going forward, she wanted limited contact with the Stewarts. For his part, Gage was just glad they'd made it through the evening, though his thoughts kept circling back to the sullen look on Fallon's face and whether the chill between them would ever thaw.

"Can you help me with this?" Fallon asked Gage the following Saturday evening. It had been a tense few days since Thanksgiving and Fallon was hoping the ice would thaw between them. They were getting ready for a hospital fund-raiser where the crème de la crème would be in attendance. She would have to shine tonight. The Givenchy gown she'd chosen had sequins from top to bottom along with dramatic layers of silver and gunmetal fringe. It would certainly help draw attention to her and Gage. It fit perfectly with the nights' Roaring Twenties theme and, with her hair swept in a sophisticated updo, Fallon looked like a modern-day flapper.

"Of course." Gage came up behind her and studied her with his hawklike gaze for several moments. She froze, her breath jamming in her throat. Then he zipped up the dress and shocked her when he planted a kiss on her bare shoulder. The hairs on the back of her neck rose to attention and every muscle in her body tensed as the earthy, sensual scent of him slammed into her senses.

Gage hadn't touched her in over a month since their argument over her not being in the mood. For her, it had been as simple as needing space, but for Gage it was as if she'd mortally wounded him with her rejection and he'd avoided her ever since. Fallon had known Gage was upset—hurt, even—but she hadn't expected him to pull away from her so completely. Despite their lack of intimacy, they still played their newlywed role by attending charity functions, polo matches and art gallery openings where Gage could rub shoulders with high society. It was going rather nicely because he'd picked up several new clients.

The distance was palpable. When they did manage to sit together for a meal, there was an ever-present underlying tension between them. Fallon didn't know how to clear the hurdle and get back to how they'd been when he couldn't get enough of her. She literally ached with unrequited feelings because now she knew what she'd been missing all those years in the bedroom. She was addicted to Gage and she needed a hit, badly.

"I have something for you." Fallon realized he'd moved away while she'd been daydreaming about him. And how could she not? Tonight he was wearing a black, three-piece, pin-striped tuxedo with black wing-tipped shoes. He'd found a vintage fedora to complete the look. He looked every bit a gangster.

He handed her a large box imprinted with the Tiffany's logo. "What's this?" She glanced up at him.

"Open it."

She did as he instructed. Nestled inside the velvet cushion was the most stunning diamond teardrop necklace she'd ever seen.

Gage unclasped it and stepped in behind her to place

it on her neck. How had he known this would comple-
ment the deep V of the dress so perfectly?

She touched the large diamond pendant. "It's beautiful."

"Just like you."

Fallon glanced into the mirror to find Gage's
brandy-colored eyes raking her boldly. She hadn't seen
that intense flare of attraction in his eyes in so long,
her heart jolted. Did it mean he still wanted her? "So
is this a truce?" she asked hopefully. "Because if not,
I'd like it to be."

Gage offered her a smile, which had been rare of
late. "Yes, let's consider it one. Now, c'mon, we should
go. We don't want to be late."

"No, we wouldn't want that." Fallon knew making
an impression tonight was important to Gage after his
humble beginnings. She would do everything in her
power to ensure the evening went well.

About forty minutes later their limousine pulled up
in front of the Four Seasons. It had taken them some
time because of the barrage of limousines filling the
streets, but eventually they disembarked and headed
inside. The venue décor was vintage art deco with a
black-and-gold color scheme that was pure glitz and
glam. There was even a photo booth so guests could
grab a fedora, flapper hat, feather boa or fake gun and
have their picture taken.

Fallon made her way around the room introducing
Gage. Everyone was polite and charming, inquiring
about their wedding and how they were enjoying married life. They even ran into her parents.

Her father gave her a hug while her mother blew her air kisses. "Don't want to ruin my makeup, darling," she purred. "You're looking well. Married life agrees with you. I love the gown. Givenchy, right?"

Trust her mother to know every designer. "That's right."

"But the true masterpiece is this diamond." Nora Stewart had no qualms about lifting the stone off Fallon's chest and admiring it. She glanced at Gage. "You outdid yourself."

"Thank you," he replied.

With that brief exchange, her mother grabbed her father's arm and continued on her socializing trek.

"Fallon? Omigod! As I live and breathe," a rather loud woman exclaimed from behind them.

Fallon spun on her heels to find Dani Collins a few feet away. She hadn't seen the buxom petite blonde since her parents had carted her away from Austin to boarding school all because she'd taken Dani's advice and tried to seduce Gage. Listening to Dani and their friend Millicent had been the reason why Fallon had ended up in Gage's room. Liquid encouragement of the alcoholic variety had also played a role.

"Dani Collins."

Dani smiled, showing a large, toothy grin. "I haven't seen you in ages." She pulled Fallon into an awkward hug. "Where have you been hiding yourself?"

"I've been working at my family's company, Stewart Technologies."

"Work?" Dani chuckled. "I would have thought you'd marry a filthy rich husband like your mama wanted before you ever worked your pretty little fingers to the bone." She held up Fallon's left hand. When her eyes landed on the six-carat ring, they nearly bugged out. "Wait a second, it looks like you have landed one."

A flicker of apprehension coursed through Fallon. "Yes, I'm married. You may remember him." She turned to Gage, who'd stepped away momentarily into another circle of partygoers. She touched his shoulder and he came forward. "Dani, this is my husband. Gage Campbell."

"What?" Dani's hand flew to her mouth. "You married the stable boy!" she shrieked.

Everyone around them turned to stare. The murderous look on Gage's face told Fallon that Dani had aroused his old fears and insecurities. Fallon could feel the deep red flush rising up to claim her cheeks.

"First of all, lower your voice, Dani," Fallon snapped. "Second, Gage is no stable boy. He's a grown man—"

But she never got to finish her sentence because Gage stepped in. "Who is, as you put it, Dani, filthy rich. So yes, I'm more than capable of looking after what's mine." His arm circled Fallon's waist. "Now if you'll excuse us…"

The lights blinked, indicating the event was about to begin. Fallon felt Gage's fingertips at her elbow as he guided her to their assigned table. He held her chair out and she sat. It was all so civilized, but when he deliberately brushed his fingers across her shoulders, Fallon shivered. *Had he intended to elicit a response?* She was sure he was upset over Dani's obnoxious comment from earlier. Tonight was his night to show society he'd arrived, and could Dani's outburst have marred that?

Once he took his seat beside her, Fallon leaned over. "You okay?" She watched him closely.

He winked but then sat with his back ramrod-straight and turned to face the front of the room. Fallon did the same, worried how the remainder of the evening would go.

Gage was fuming. Outwardly he portrayed the image of self-made millionaire, but inside he was still that twelve-year-old boy who'd come to live with his mother when she became the maid on a big estate. The same young boy who'd turned into a stable hand that silly rich socialites like Dani Collins made fun of or bedded to show they were living dangerously.

Fallon was special. He'd watched her grow up from a spirited young girl into an attractive teenager with stunning hazel-gray eyes. He had been drawn to her. It's why he'd humored her, talked to her and let her follow him around. That night he'd thought to teach her a lesson, but it had morphed into one hell of a kiss. Gage had been ill prepared for the chemistry that had exploded between them. He'd ended it before they'd gone too far.

Yet in the eyes of Dani and some like her, he would always be a stable boy and that stuck in his craw. Gage lifted a hand to catch the attention of the waiter and requested a whiskey. He needed something stronger, less smooth than his usual brandy. Something to take the edge off to ensure he got through this night in one piece.

Three whiskeys and several hours later, Gage felt relaxed. The evening was nearly over. The hospital raised the requisite amount of money needed thanks to a last-minute, million-dollar donation from him, which had shocked the entire room, including his wife sitting beside him.

When the band finally struck up some lively tunes, Gage was ready to alleviate some tension. Fallon returned from freshening up in the bathroom with her mother and looked quite delectable in her metallic flapper dress. He couldn't wait to take it off her later and he'd be damned if she'd refuse him. He'd seen the look in her eyes tonight and knew she still hungered for him.

He stood and held out a hand. "Dance with me?"

Fallon slid her hand into his and allowed him to lead her to the dance floor, which was already crowded with couples. The song was a slow Etta James melody called "At Last." Gage eased his arms around Fallon's warm body and pulled her tightly to him. Then he leaned his forehead against hers and whispered, "I've missed you."

She was silent for several beats and Gage wondered if she'd heard him, but then she responded. "I've missed you, too."

Her words were like a match to his lust and Gage pressed his body closer so she could feel how he was straining in his trousers. "Will you let me have you tonight?" he growled.

"Yes."

Yes. The word had never sounded lovelier to Gage's ears. And once the song ended, he quickly danced them off the floor and back to the table so Fallon could grab her clutch and gloves. They were nearly at the door when once again Dani stepped in front of them.

She was weaving back and forth, looking like she'd had one too many drinks. "I have to hand it to you, Fallon. You certainly know how to pick them. Maybe I, too, should have gotten it on with our stable boy. Maybe then he would have become rich and famous and come back to bail my company out of trouble."

"You don't know what you're talking about," Fallon answered, a warning in her tone.

"D-don't I?" Dani slurred. "From what I hear, your daddy's company was about to go belly-up, until stable boy here—" Dani eyed Gage up and down "—came along. Did you finally have to put out?"

Fallon's eyes narrowed. "You're a witch, you know that?"

"I might be, but I'm a rich one," Dani returned.

"That no man wants," Fallon snorted. "It's no wonder you're alone. I, on the other hand, am not. I'm going home with *my man* and let me tell you something, Dani. He's the fantasy in bed we all thought he was." She didn't wait for another of Dani's catty responses. Fallon grabbed Gage's hand and stormed out of the ballroom.

"That was hot!" Gage couldn't help but comment. He loved Fallon's outburst. This was the second time she'd defended him tonight. Whatever residual anger he'd felt from the last month faded. Fallon was truly in his corner.

"Good." She stared at him boldly. "Because I need you bad. So, buckle up. It's going to be a long night."

A smile curved his lips. He was ready for whatever Fallon had in store because they had a month to make up for.

They didn't make it very far into the penthouse because Gage pressed Fallon against the wall of the living room as soon as they arrived. Then his lips found hers in the dark and he kissed her hard. Their mouths fused together in a tangle of tongues. Fallon didn't know who moved first. She knew her hand was sneaking under his tuxedo to push off the jacket. Gage pulled away long enough to shrug it off, undo his tie and unbutton his shirt. When her eyes landed on his flat brown nipples, she leaned forward and explored the salty taste of him.

She had a growing need to see him naked. When the buttons were finally free, Gage ripped the shirt off. Only minutes after they'd entered the apartment, he was naked from the waist up while she was still fully clothed. Gage reached for her, hauling her to him. He reached behind her, fumbling with the zipper on the back of her dress, but it wouldn't give.

"Damnation!" he cursed and then pulled one strap and then the other over her arms. Her breasts popped free and his mouth was on them in seconds, reducing her to writhing ecstasy. They were tight and puckered at his mouth and touch alone. Fallon's mind skittered as her insides fisted tight with need. She couldn't think of anything but Gage and how much she wanted him. She didn't care what anyone else thought; she would die if she didn't feel him inside her *now*.

She was sure Gage felt the same way because his

erection had thickened. She reached between them to undo his belt and zipper, but he pushed her hands aside. In one fell swoop he pulled down his trousers and briefs and kicked away his clothes. He was gloriously naked and Fallon looked her fill. Then he was back, sliding his hands into her hair and kissing her. His hands roamed lower, hiking up her dress until it was bunched around her waist.

"Wrap your legs around me," he instructed roughly.

He didn't have to tell her twice. Gage hitched her up, resting her back against the wall, and Fallon wrapped her legs around him. Holding her with one arm, he reached between them to push aside her thong and slide a finger between her moist folds. She was already wet for him, as she always was, and without preamble he widened his stance and surged upward inside her.

Fallon had never felt so full, so taken, so possessed. She slid her arms around his neck and Gage thrust higher. Her breath hitched. He withdrew and thrust back in, this time going even deeper.

"Yes, Gage, oh, yes," she moaned and her head fell back against the wall. She closed her eyes, amazed at the fullness of having Gage inside her once again. Starbursts of blinding light exploded behind her eyes as pleasure washed over her.

"Look at me, Fallon."

She opened her eyes and found Gage staring at her. He cupped her bottom tighter in his palms and pushed higher. He was intent on pulling her apart, on dismantling every single one of her defenses. He accomplished his goal with single-minded purpose as he increased his rhythm and drove into her over and over.

"Gage…" Fallon's body grew taut and soon she felt herself clench around him as spasms overtook her. She heard his release in the distance as they both finally broke free.

Fourteen

"I have a lead for you," Gage's attorney told him over the phone the next morning. "The final shares you need to give you a majority in Stewart Technologies."

"What was that?" Gage asked absentmindedly. He'd been daydreaming about Fallon's uninhibited response last night. He should be satisfied he could bring her to that kind of climax, but he hadn't been unaffected, either. He had feelings for her, probably always had since he'd seen her fall off her horse when she was eight.

Being with Fallon had injected his life with meaning and made him feel emotions he'd never allowed himself to feel. The past two months had shown him she wasn't the strong woman she portrayed to the world. She was passionate. Vulnerable, even. There were so many layers to his beautiful wife he hadn't considered. He'd been so intent on taking her to bed, to claim what he hadn't taken sixteen years ago and unleash the chemistry between them, he'd failed to see the consequences of his actions. He was falling for his wife. *Hard.*

"I said I have a lock on those shares you need," his attorney repeated, clearing his fog. "Since the company is rebounding, stock prices are slowly starting to rise. You'll want to get these now, while you can."

Gage's chest tightened and guilt settled in his stomach as the heavy weight of what he'd been doing registered. He needed someone to absolve him of the guilt, to tell him he what he'd done was right. But that wasn't going to happen. If Fallon ever found out his true motives behind marrying her, it would crush her. She'd been so happy the last few weeks as she'd pulled Stewart Technologies from the brink of disaster. The projects she'd been working on would be coming to market in a couple of months. They were the brainchild of her new head of development and Fallon was excited to see what lay ahead.

"Are you ready to pull the trigger?"

A throb pulsed at Gage's temple and he massaged it with his fingertips, trying to alleviate the pressure, but nothing was going to do that. His feelings for Fallon ran deep and he was conflicted as to what to do next. "I—I…"

"If you don't act now, someone could swoop in and pick them up. You have to move."

Gage sighed. He couldn't allow anyone else to get those shares. They had to stay in the family. On the other hand, this enormous deceit weighed heavily on him. He would be crossing the line when he did this.

"Go ahead and purchase them."

"I'm on it. I'll let you know when it's a done deal."

"Thank you." Gage ended the call. He sat back in his seat and rubbed a hand across his brow. There was no denying the emotion he'd never wanted to claim; it was there mocking him because he'd thought he could skirt it. Thought he didn't need it. He certainly hadn't needed it before. Why? Because none of those women had been Fallon.

Yet, because of her, he'd wanted more. To *be* more. And he'd accomplished that. But with it had come the all-consuming rage and quest for revenge. He now had the tools, the final nail in the coffin to get his ultimate revenge against the Stewarts, but it would cost him the woman he loved.

"What should I expect tonight?" Gage asked Fallon as they drove to the restaurant to meet Ayden and his fiancée, Maya, for dinner. "The firing squad?"

"Don't be so melodramatic." Fallon smoothed down her skirt.

"C'mon, Fallon." Gage took his eyes off the road to glance at her. "I know your brother doesn't like me. It was obvious at the wedding."

Gage recalled the killer look Ayden had given him when they'd been introduced. Ayden had warned Gage to take care of his sister or else.

"He doesn't know you. Give him a chance," Fallon said, obviously attempting to ease Gage's mind.

"If he affords me the same, I will," Gage responded, turning his eyes to the road again. He knew how important this dinner was to Fallon. She was forging a bond with her brother and he didn't want to get in the way, not when he wasn't on even footing himself.

"Good."

They pulled into the restaurant's valet parking twenty minutes later. Gage came around and helped Fallon out of the car, then laced his fingers through hers as they walked inside. The maître d' led them to a corner table where Ayden and Maya were already seated. Gage could see why Ayden had fallen for his fiancée. She was striking, with her mass of curly hair and flawless brown skin.

Ayden rose when they approached. He came over and kissed both of Fallon's cheeks and offered Gage a hand. Gage shook it before scooting Fallon into a chair across from them.

"Glad you both could join us," Ayden said. He glanced at Maya. "We're eager to get to know you."

"As are we," Gage answered. He offered them a smile.

"How about some wine?" Ayden asked. "I took the liberty of ordering a bottle of red."

"We would love some, thank you." Fallon patted his thigh. She knew Gage liked ordering their wine himself.

"How's married life?" Maya inquired. "I can't believe you two beat me and Ayden down the aisle."

"It certainly wasn't a shotgun wedding," Gage replied.

"Then what was the rush?" Ayden asked. "Were you afraid Fallon might change her mind?"

Gage felt Fallon's fury beside him rather than saw it. She didn't appreciate her brother's inappropriate comment any more than he did, so he reminded himself Ayden was merely concerned for Fallon's well-being. "No, I wasn't afraid. I knew Fallon would honor the commitment she'd made to be my wife." He reached for her hand and brought it to his lips.

"How is married life treating you?" Maya asked. Bless her heart, Ayden's fiancée was keeping the evening cordial.

"It's going well, thank you, Maya," Fallon responded. "Actually, better than I'd imagined. Gage even manages to keep the toilet seat down."

Fallon's joke lightened the mood and everyone began to relax. But Gage could see Ayden watching his every move. Could he see what Gage had yet to share with Fallon—that he loved her?

Fallon was overjoyed the dinner was turning around. It had started off rocky with Ayden giving Gage the death stare. She knew her brother wasn't happy about her arranged marriage to Gage, but he was going to have to live with it for another four months.

Her breath caught in her throat when she realized two months had already come and gone. The first month with Gage had been sheer bliss. The way they'd connected on such an elemental level had surprised her. All her life she'd been searching for that elusive connection with another human being. She'd found it in Gage; it was as if he fit perfectly into the slot. With each passing day and all the intimacy they'd shared, it became harder to keep her true feelings from bubbling to the surface. It's why she'd pushed him away, making the last month hard. When Gage had felt rejected by her, he'd kept her at a distance, physically as well as emotionally.

His response had hurt, but she'd had to withdraw to save herself the pain she knew was coming. However, not being with him had hurt far worse than anything she could have imagined. Last night after the event, they'd given in and finally made love. It had felt so good and oh so right. That was why she'd felt in a good place to accept Ayden's dinner invite.

"Gage is treating you well, which I'm glad to see," Ayden whispered in her ear when they'd retired to the lounge to listen to a jazz quartet. Gage and Maya were engaged in a lively discussion on the latest mayoral candidate, while Ayden and Fallon stepped onto the terrace for a private conversation and some fresh air because Fallon had felt a bit queasy.

"He is."

"Is the fresh air helping?" Ayden asked.

Fallon nodded and inhaled deeply. The last week or so she hadn't had much of an appetite. And after seeing the crème brûlée Gage had ordered for dessert, she'd felt sick to her stomach.

"After hearing his story, I realize I misjudged him," Ayden said after a moment.

During the meal Gage had shared the story of his inauspicious start in life, from never knowing his father to being raised on Stewart Manor to branching out on his own after college to find success. Fallon could see how impressed Ayden was by Gage's determination. He respected her husband because he knew what it was like to make something out of nothing.

"I told you not to worry."

Ayden snorted. "It's an older brother's prerogative to worry, Fallon. It would be different if you'd married for love, but you didn't."

Color drained from Fallon's face and Ayden leaned in. "Omigod! You're in love with him, aren't you?" He glanced in Gage's direction and Fallon followed Ayden's gaze. Her husband was watching them and smiling.

She quickly turned around and tugged on Ayden's sleeve, leading him farther away. "Lower your voice, please."

Ayden looked down at her. His hazel-gray eyes pierced hers. "Does he know?"

Fallon shook her head. "And I don't want him to know."

"Why the hell not? I see the way he looks at you, Fallon. There's something there."

"Lust," she replied. "Lust is all that's there, Ayden. We're compatible in the bedroom."

"Are you sure? Because I would beg to differ."

"Trust me, I know," Fallon responded. "Let's keep this between us, okay? I don't want him to know."

"You don't want me to know what?" came the deep masculine voice from behind Fallon. Her heart thumped erratically. What had he heard?

"How I'm not that big a fan of jazz, but that it's your cup of tea," Fallon responded, turning to her husband with a smile.

Gage's arm snaked around her waist. "Babe, you should have told me. We could have gone someplace else."

She shrugged. "It's fine. Ayden said he'd been wanting to come here for a while, too. Isn't that right?" She glanced up at her brother for support.

Ayden grinned. "That's right. So let's go back to our seats. The quartet is back."

The evening ended with Fallon and Gage saying their goodbyes and planning on another double date with Ayden and Maya. Afterward, in the car, Fallon was happy to hear Gage had enjoyed himself.

"That went well," he said on the drive home. "I like Ayden."

"You sound surprised."

"I thought he was going to treat me like your parents. Like I wasn't good enough for you."

Fallon realized how deep Gage's past wounds were when it came to being accepted. How her and her friends' treatment of him had had a profound effect on who he was today.

"But he didn't treat me that way. Instead he treated me with respect and I feel the same about him. What Ayden has been able to accomplish without any help from your father is nothing short of amazing."

Fallon beamed with pride. "He's pretty great, isn't he?"

"Yeah, must be something in the genes." Gage glanced in her direction.

A swell of rightness filled Fallon. If they had a *real* marriage, this would be the start of a great beginning for their family, but they didn't and it wasn't. What was she going to do at the end of six months when it was time to say goodbye?

"Fallon?" She heard the question in his voice. "You got silent on me all of a sudden. You okay?"

She nodded but deep down she was afraid of losing him.

Fifteen

"Why did I agree to do this?" Gage wondered aloud as he helped Theo drill nails into the new storage shed behind his home.

"Because you owe me one," his friend responded.

"What for?"

"For telling you about the Stewarts' plight," Theo replied. He glanced in the direction of the house where Fallon was talking with his girlfriend, Amanda, whom he'd started seeing a few weeks ago. "If I hadn't, you wouldn't be married now."

Gage laughed. "If I recall, you told me I was out of my mind to consider marrying my sworn enemy."

Theo shrugged. "Who knew you'd be the happiest I've seen you in years? You're a changed man, my friend."

"How so?"

"Lighter. Happy. And it's all because of the woman in there." He pointed to Fallon, whom Gage could see through the oversize kitchen window.

"She's certainly made an impact."

"Admit it, Gage. You have feelings for the woman. Probably always did, which is why it was so easy for you to make that offer."

Gage knew Theo was right. On some deeper level, he'd always wanted Fallon even when she'd been off-limits and too young to know any better.

"So what now?"

"What do you mean?"

"Didn't you only agree to a six-month arrangement? What happens when your time is up and Fallon wants out?"

Gage's eyes narrowed. He knew he was putting his head in the sand, but he refused to consider it. Fallon was happy with them, with their life. He was certain if he presented her with the opportunity to stay with him, she wouldn't leave. "I don't think that's going to happen, Theo."

"She signed documents. She doesn't owe you a thing."

"She owes herself," Gage responded quickly. "She owes it to us to see how this plays out. Instead of turning tail and running away."

"Sounds like you've gotten very comfortable being a married man," Theo noted. "I hope this doesn't blow up in your face. I mean, what happens when Fallon finds out your true motives for marrying her? How do you think she'll feel?"

Gage knew the answer. "She'll feel betrayed." She wouldn't be angry. She'd hate him for stealing her birthright like Henry did to Ayden. And it scared the living daylights out of him. But he was in so deep, there was no way out. By purchasing those final shares, he was sealing his fate and setting them on a collision course. But Gage was powerless to stop it.

"Then for God's sake, come clean with her, man. Tell her what you've done and maybe—maybe—you can work it out."

Gage stiffened. "I can't. I could lose her."

"You can lose her if you don't," Theo stated.

Gage looked toward the window and found Fallon watching and waving at him. His heart turned in his chest and Gage knew he would do anything to keep her.

"That was fun," Fallon said when she and Gage returned to the penthouse later that evening. He'd been very quiet during dinner and, on the ride back, she wondered if he and Theo had had some sort of disagreement outside.

"Yeah, it was good," Gage said absentmindedly as he headed to the kitchen and grabbed a beer out of the fridge. He twisted the top off, took a pull and leaned against the counter.

Fallon removed her leather jacket and boots and followed him, watching him closely. The last couple of months she'd picked up on Gage's mood. She knew when something was on his mind. "You can talk to me about whatever it is that's upsetting you."

"I'm fine."

Fallon nodded. He was stonewalling her and she didn't like it. "Suit yourself." She spun around and walked into the master suite. She was removing her jewelry and placing it in the holder when Gage came marching in behind her.

"We don't have to share our feelings all the time, Fallon," he snarled. "It's all right to keep something to ourselves."

"So you admit you have secrets?" Fallon responded, spinning around to face him. "That you're keeping something from me?"

"I never said that."

Her eyes narrowed. "You didn't have to. Because your answer just said it all."

"Damn it, Fallon. What do you want from me?"

"Everything! Nothing." She shook her head. "Hell, I don't know, Gage. I blindly agreed to this marriage to save my family's company but I had no idea what it would be like, how I would feel..." Her voice trailed off.

"And how do you feel?"

She stared at him incredulously. "You want me to lay my heart bare when you're not willing to do the same?" She shook her head. "I don't think so."

She moved away and headed into the bathroom to brush her teeth, but Gage was right there. "I want to know."

"Well, that's too bad. Because I have my own secrets."

His face turned to stone. "You're saying that to get back at me."

He was wrong. The last couple of weeks she'd felt off, as if something was wrong. She hadn't had much of an appetite and was nauseous the last few mornings. It was odd. When she'd spoken to Theo's girlfriend, she'd asked Fallon about her last period. That's when it dawned on Fallon: she hadn't had one since she and Gage were married. She'd been so enraptured with her husband it had slipped her mind. Amanda had gently suggested she get a pregnancy test to find out for sure, but Fallon was afraid.

A baby?

She was on the pill to guarantee there would be no strings once the marriage was over. *What could have happened?* Had she missed a day? A rising panic threatened to overtake her. Guilt. Regret. Fear. Love. Fallon was feeling too many emotions to share a potential pregnancy with Gage. Not until she was sure.

"Fallon." Gage's light brown gaze sharpened as he drew near. "What is it? What don't I know?"

"Don't turn this around on me, Gage," Fallon responded tightly. "You said you want to keep feelings and emotions to yourself. I merely expressed I'll do the same. If you don't like it, that's tough."

She knew before he moved that he was going to kiss her. Kiss away her insolence. And she would let him because a hot sea of need always seemed to be just below the surface with them.

"Don't think this changes anything," Fallon murmured before his lips covered hers and his hands began skimming her body. His fingers tugged on the narrow straps of her sundress until they loosened and he could tug it to her waist.

His response was a raw, shaken laughter. "Duly noted. Now, are you going to let me love you?"

"Yes…" Gage's mouth left hers and his tongue began trailing an erotic path of fire from her throat, neck and shoulders to her breast. When he reached one chocolate nipple, he lowered his head and took the turgid peak in his mouth. She released an audible sigh and gave in.

Long moments later, when they lay spent and wrapped in each other arms, Fallon stared up at the ceiling. They'd shared something special, magical even, and emotions swelled in her.

Gage seemed to sense it, too. As if reading her mind, he tried to verbalize it. "Fallon," he said huskily. "Fallon, I—I—"

Fallon touched his cheek because she understood how hard it was to say those three words out loud. So she said them to herself. *I love you.* And if they had created a baby, she would love it because it was a part of him. It would mean they would be inextricably tied together for years. Was she prepared for that? She knew she loved him, but it couldn't be just her. It took two people fully committed to make a marriage work, let alone to parent a child. Fallon wasn't sure they had what it took for the long haul.

Fallon had a splitting headache. She'd felt not quite right all day.

Lunch with her mother hadn't helped. Nora griped

about the meager allowance she was being given for living expenses. Fallon had tried to politely explain she needed to curb her spending habits. The company was not out of the woods. Gage's influx of cash had certainly helped, but it was up to Fallon to get them back on course.

Nora hadn't liked what she'd said. She'd yelled and pitched a fit, accusing Fallon of being unfair. "You have a rich husband now. I would think you would be looking out for your mother. Instead you're selfish and want all the money to yourself."

Fallon had curtly reminded Nora she didn't live off Gage and wasn't going to take another dime from him just because Nora couldn't control her impulses. They'd ended the lunch on an unpleasant note. Fallon was thankful to return to the office and had planned to lie down, but then she'd received an urgent call from Ayden.

"Fallon, I have to see you. Can you meet me?"

Fallon agreed and was anxiously awaiting his visit. That's when the stomach cramps started. He'd sounded urgent, as if it was a matter of life and death, and she didn't have a clue what it might be. She hoped everything was okay with him and Maya.

When Ayden arrived dressed in his usual attire of suit and tie with designer shoes, he looked serious and his jaw was tight.

"Ayden, what on earth is the matter?" Fallon asked, closing the door behind him. She motioned him to the sofa in her office. "Please have a seat."

"I have some news and you're not going to like what I have to say," Ayden replied, sitting.

Fallon sucked in a breath and willed the cramps away. She joined him on the couch. "Hit me with it. It's already been a bad day. It can't get much worse."

Ayden peered at her strangely.

"For Christ's sake, Ayden. You're scaring me. What is it?"

He inhaled deeply. "I want you to know it gives me no pleasure in doing this."

Fallon searched his face for a sign but couldn't find one. A sense of foreboding came over her that the happiness she'd found with Gage could be at risk.

"You know I run an investment firm and many people come to me to manage their portfolios."

"Damn it, Ayden. Don't beat around the bush. Just tell me."

"I'm breaking a confidence in sharing this with you, but while reviewing one of my client's portfolios, I learned he'd offloaded a substantial amount of Stewart Technologies' stock."

A sharp pain hit Fallon deep in the pit of her stomach. She tried not to react, but it was significantly more than any of the cramps from earlier that day. Still, she masked the pain. She had to know what was happening. "Go on."

"There was one purchaser of the stock, Fallon." He paused several beats. "It was Gage. He used a holding company so it couldn't immediately be traced back to him."

"No, no." Fallon shook her head and tears sprung to her eyes. This couldn't be happening. Not now. "Are you sure it's Gage? Maybe you could be wrong."

"I wish I were, but when I noticed this holding company buying all of my client's stock, I decided to do some digging. That's when I found out Stewart Technologies' stock is owned by several different holding companies. So I dug deeper into the paperwork of each company and lo and behold, Gage was the president of each of those firms. Despite your claim that Gage's incentive for marrying you was acceptance by the upper echelon, I never entirely bought it and now I know why. He wanted Stewart Technologies. And he has it, Fallon. Based on his last stock purchase, he has the majority share in the company."

Majority share.

Another cramp seized her and she clutched her stomach.

Gage has a majority stake in my company.

He could take it over at any time. Exercise his rights and boot her out of the company. Steal her birthright like Henry had done to Ayden all those years ago. By essentially not claiming Ayden as his son, their father hadn't allowed Ayden the chance to run the company. The shoe was on the other foot; now she knew what it was like to be in her big brother's shoes.

She rose even though the pain was excruciating. A cold sweat was forming on her forehead.

What a fool she'd been to believe a word that came out of Gage's mouth. This must have been his end game all along. Ayden was right. Gage didn't want acceptance. He wanted vengeance and he'd attained it at her expense. He must have laughed at how gullible and naïve she was. They just happened to be compatible in the bedroom and he'd gotten his jollies off.

"Fallon, are you all right?" Ayden was immediately on his feet and rushing over to her. "You're looking very pale."

"I—I can't." The pain was intense now and she clutched her stomach.

"I'm taking you the hospital." Within seconds Ayden lifted her into her arms and was striding for the door.

Gage stared down at the paper in his hands. This was it. He finally had a fifty-one-percent ownership stake in Stewart Technologies. After all these years he was finally in a position of power over Henry Stewart, the man who'd put him and his mother out on the street with no home, no job and only the clothes on their backs.

He'd blamed himself for what happened to his mother. Perhaps if he'd ignored Fallon, hadn't shown any interest, she would have never come to their cottage. Who knows where life would have led him if he hadn't been spurred to succeed? If he hadn't pushed himself to do more, be more, so no one could ever look down on him again?

Sharing one unforgettable kiss with Fallon had been a defining moment that had changed the course of his life. But now time had passed and he could see it had been for the better. He'd achieved the highest levels of success on Wall Street. He could afford anything and everything he'd ever wanted or dreamed of.

But what would it all mean if he was alone with no

one to share it with? Getting involved with the Stewarts two months ago had altered his life once again. Marrying Fallon was the single best decision he'd ever made. The life they shared together was so rich, so full, so exciting, so passionate. Gage would never get tired of her eternal optimism, her bright smile, her easy nature. She truly was a rare diamond.

Quite honestly, she was everything he hadn't known he'd been looking for. He loved her. And he wanted *theirs* to be a real marriage. Not a temporary one. And although he excelled at managing people and situations, tonight he was going to be honest and tell her he'd been foolish thinking revenge was the answer. It wasn't. He was going tell Fallon he loved her.

"Fallon, oh, thank God." Ayden came into the hospital room and wrapped his arms around her. "Thank God you're okay. I was so worried. And the doctors—" he glanced behind him at the door "—wouldn't tell me anything. Even though I'm your brother, I'm not on your approved list to receive medical information, so they wouldn't—"

Ayden stopped rambling when he saw the tears streaming down her cheeks. "Fallon, what is it? Is it something serious? What can I do?"

Fallon laughed without humor. "There's nothing you or anyone else can do."

Ayden's eyes grew large with fear and he began grabbing at his tie as if it was too tight around his neck. "Is it bad?"

"If you mean being pregnant by a man who doesn't

love you and used you for revenge against your family?" Fallon asked. "Then, yes, it's bad."

"Pregnant?"

The word hung in the air like the albatross it was. Fallon felt it around her neck and there was nothing she could do about it. Deep down, she'd known it was true, but had been afraid to take the test. Well, the stomach cramps and spotting had led her *here*, to the hospital, getting medication to help prevent a miscarriage.

"Yes," Fallon replied. "I'm pregnant."

Ayden rubbed his bald head and then turned to face her. "Does Gage know?"

"No."

"Did you?"

Fallon locked gazes with her brother. "I suspected." She wiped at the tears she couldn't stop. It had to be hormones—she hardly ever cried. "But... I didn't want to believe it, you know? We signed a six-month marriage contract. A baby wasn't part of the agreement."

"But it's here now."

"Your point?"

"You're going to have to face this, Fallon. Face Gage," Ayden responded.

"After everything he's done? How can I?" Fallon sniffed. She knew the truth now. The only reason he'd married her was for revenge. To stick it to her, to her father, for the wrongs against him and his mother.

And he'd achieved his goal.

He'd also single-handedly ruined any chance of saving their marriage. Of their being a family one day. He'd made a fool of her and she would never forgive him.

Fallon inhaled sharply. Her mama bear instincts kicked in and she rubbed her stomach, willing her nerves to subside. Gage may have won this round. Fallon hoped he enjoyed it because she was walking away with the most precious gift of all. Their child. And he would have no part of its life. She would see to that.

Sixteen

Fallon was in the hospital.

Gage's heart thumped in his chest as he frantically made his way there. When he'd stopped by to pick her up from work, her assistant, Chelsea, had informed him she'd experienced stomach pains and Ayden had taken her to the hospital. Gage was terrified. What could be wrong? Fallon was the picture of health. In their short time together he'd seen how she took very good care of herself. She ate right and went to the gym. Working out with his wife one of his favorite pastimes. She was a great sparring partner, though it was difficult to focus when she wore workout capris and one of those sports bras that bared her midriff.

He was terrified something was terribly wrong.
But what?

As soon as he pulled up at the valet stand, Gage quickly dispensed with his keys and rushed inside. After finding her room number, he took off running down the hall. What had stunned him was when the nurse had told him she was in the maternity ward. *Why in the hell would she be there?* The ride seemed interminable but eventually the elevator stopped and he disembarked. He found her room and strode to the door. When he arrived, she was sitting up in bed and Ayden was in a nearby chair.

"Thank God, you're all right," Gage said, hastening toward her. He bent his head to kiss her but she held up her hand and blocked him.

"Don't even try it." She lurched away from him as if he were contaminated with some virus.

Gage stepped back and stared at Fallon in confusion. He didn't understand the look of disgust on her face. He glanced at Ayden, but he had a stony expression. "Would either of you care to tell me what's going on? When Chelsea told me you were in the hospital, I was worried sick. You have no idea the crazy scenarios that were running through my mind. Do they know what's wrong? Why are you here in the maternity ward?"

Fallon turned to Ayden. "Do you mind giving us some time alone?"

Ayden glanced in Gage's direction and the dirty look he gave him told Gage that he was not pleased to see him. "Are you sure? I can stay behind."

She shook her head. "No, Gage and I need to have this conversation in private."

Ayden nodded and got to his feet. He leaned down

and pressed a kiss against her forehead. "I'll be outside the door if you need me."

She attempted a half smile. "Thank you."

After giving Gage another fiery look that could have melted ice, Ayden left the room and closed the door.

Gage again moved toward the bed. "Fallon, please. Tell me what's wrong. What happened?"

She glared at him. "I don't know, Gage. Why don't you tell me since you decided to stab me in the back?"

"Pardon?"

Her hand slashed through the air. "Don't act coy. Now's your time to exact the revenge you've been plotting for months. I'm a sitting duck. Take your best shot."

A knot formed in his stomach. Surely Fallon couldn't know about the shares of Stewart Technologies' stock he'd acquired. *Could she?* "What are you talking about?"

"Really? Really?" She raised her eyebrows. "You're not going to admit it? You're going to make me spell it out for you? All right then, Gage. I'll bite. One question. How long have you been conspiring to take over my company?" She folded her arms across her chest and waited for his response.

She knew.

"Fallon, I can explain." His voice was low, tense.

"Ha." She laughed without humor. "I seriously doubt that." Her voice was tight. "But go ahead and try me."

Gage had an overwhelming urge to wrap his arms around her and hold her close. In the bed, she looked small and fragile wearing the hospital-issued gown, her hair hanging limply around her shoulders. Even her hazel-gray eyes seemed cloudy. Yet her voice was strong and fierce. He moved past her and walked to the window overlooking the street.

When he remained silent she said, "Well?" Her voice was cold and distant.

He spun around to face her. "I won't lie. I've been acquiring Stewart Technologies' stock for a couple months."

"So you admit it?"

He took a deep breath and nodded. "I was angry, Fallon. I wanted retribution for how your family treated us sixteen years ago. Your father threw us out with nothing but the clothes on our backs. He left us with nothing. No clothes. No money. Not even a reference for my mother, who'd worked for him for nearly a decade. You have no idea the trials and tribulations we faced starting over."

At her stone-faced silence, he continued. "I was angry. Rage coursed through my DNA and I vowed that someday I would get back at the Stewarts. After living on the estate and hearing the barbs from your wealthy friends, I recognized the reality of my life. I had to be successful. I promised myself I would elevate myself to a better station in life. One in which no one could ever treat me as anything less than an equal."

"And when did you decide to use me as a pawn in your revenge scenario?"

His gaze landed on Fallon. "You were never a pawn, Fallon. I wanted you. I've always wanted you. Even back then, when you were sixteen. But the timing wasn't right then. I had to push you away—but not before I kissed you. And it was that kiss that I've never forgotten."

"Oh, please, don't make it sound like it was more than it was. I was just a naïve girl making a play for you."

"It was more than that. It stirred something in me," Gage replied, "but I pushed it down. And after we were kicked out, I tried to forget you. And I did a good job of it with lots of women of all shapes and sizes. Beautiful women. But they weren't you, Fallon."

"Stop it, Gage. Don't act like we had some unrequited love because it doesn't ring true. You deliberately sought out retribution, against me and my family. Ayden told me everything. He told me how you've been purchasing shares of the company behind my back."

"Can you blame me?" Gage inquired testily. "I was angry. Angry about the raw deal we received."

"No, I wouldn't blame you if you hated me and my family, but I point-blank asked if you could put what happened behind you. You lied to me. Told me you could forgive but wouldn't forget." She sighed. "You let me believe…" Fallon's words trailed off.

"Believe what?" The tension that gripped her was vibrating through him, engulfing them in a volatile bubble.

"That you *cared*?" she yelled at him as her eyes swept downward. "This entire time I was drifting along in some fantasy world in which I thought you and I might actually last beyond the contract, but it was all a lie." She pierced him with her gaze. "It's all about crime and punishment with you, isn't it?"

"It may have started out that way, Fallon," Gage said. He came to sit beside her on the bed and this time she didn't move away. "But it quickly changed once I saw you again and the familiar visceral response I had to you wouldn't be denied. I admit, marriage was never my intention. I'd thought one night together would be enough and I would rid myself of this simmering attraction I felt for you. But that night in the car...you must remember how hot it was between us. We were a fuse waiting to be lit and, when we were finally together, it was incredible. More than incredible. I realized I'd grossly miscalculated my feelings."

"Feelings. We're talking about feelings," Fallon scoffed. "We've been married for two months, Gage, and this is the first time you mentioned those. But it doesn't matter because I don't believe a word you say. You've gotten what you wanted. Me in your bed, an introduction into Austin society and the Stewart family at your mercy with you calling all the shots. And now I want you out of my room and out of my life."

"Fallon...listen, I know you're upset and when you calm down we can talk rationally."

"I am rational and I want you gone. Go!"

"Not until I know you're okay," Gage responded. "You collapsed, for Christ's sake, and I'm not—" The words he'd been about to say cut off when he noticed the book on the bedside table.

What to Expect When You're Expecting.

Suddenly it became very clear to him why she was

in the maternity ward. It was the same reason she hadn't been eating much lately and had gotten sick a couple of mornings. It was why her breasts had felt fuller and more sensitive during their lovemaking.

Fallon was pregnant.

Fallon knew the moment the truth hit Gage. Color leached from his face and he looked at her. "Are you…?"

"You know the answer to that question," Fallon responded.

"How?"

Fallon shook her head. "I don't know. I was taking the pills, but apparently that's normal. Anyway, it doesn't change the facts. I'm going to have a baby."

"You mean *we're* having a baby," he replied.

"This baby is mine," Fallon stated fiercely, clutching her stomach.

His gaze zeroed in on her action. "Fallon…"

"I don't need or want you, Gage. Neither does this baby."

Gage's face was drawn and tight, and Fallon knew she'd hit a nerve.

"A child needs its father. And I won't be separated from him or her." Gage's tone was vehement.

"You have no rights," Fallon stated. "My body, my choice. And right now I choose not to have anything to do with a liar for a husband."

"You're being unreasonable. You must know this changes everything between us, Fallon. It's not black-and-white anymore."

"You mean like it was for you when you conspired against me?" Fallon sat upright in the bed. "When you mercilessly seduced me night after night until I ended up here in this bed!" She pointed downward. "You used me for your own enjoyment and amusement. What was I to you but some pampered bed-warmer you could keep handy when you had an itch that needed scratching?"

"That's not true!" he retorted hotly. "I've never treated you with anything less than respect."

Fire flashed in Fallon's eyes. "Respect. You call lying and going behind my back respect? You don't know the meaning of the word and I won't let me or my baby be a pawn in your games any longer. I want you out. Now!" she yelled.

Suddenly the door to her hospital room swung open and Ayden walked in. His eyes were laser-focused on her. "I could hear Fallon screaming down the hall. What the hell is going on?" He looked at Gage.

"Please make him leave." Fallon turned onto her side and faced the window. She couldn't bear to look at Gage. Not knowing how incredibly foolish she'd been to fall for his lies. He'd set this course of events in motion and now they'd created a life. She placed her hand over her small, rounding belly.

Ayden walked over to Gage. "I won't have you upsetting Fallon anymore, Gage. She nearly suffered a miscarriage because of your lies and machinations."

"But the baby's okay?" Gage asked.

Fallon studiously avoided looking at him. "*For now. I was having spotting and cramps. The doctor put me* on some medication that will hopefully stop them, but I need to rest and be stress-free."

"Meaning you don't want me anywhere near you? Is that it?"

"That's right," Fallon responded hotly and turned to glare at him. "You can go back to your high-profile Wall Street existence making loads of money because I don't want or need you and neither does my baby. Consider the contract we signed null and void. Gather your team of highly paid lawyers and get them to send over whatever paperwork is necessary to end this sham of a marriage."

"Fallon, you can't get rid of me that easy. Not only did we sign a contract, but I own a majority stake at Stewart Technologies."

Fallon's eyes flashed fire. "So you're threatening me?"

"No, of course not." Gage sighed. "This isn't coming out right. I want you to calm down."

"Then let me show you the exit." Ayden motioned to the door.

Gage held up his hands in surrender. "Okay. I'll leave for now, but I will be back, Fallon. It isn't over between us."

When she finally heard the door click shut, Fallon fell back against the pillows. Holding herself up, being strong in front of Gage, had zapped all her energy.

"It's all right, Fallon. You can rest now." Ayden came forward and helped make her more comfortable on the bed. "I meant what I told Gage. You need to get some sleep."

"Are you leaving?"

Ayden shook his head. "No, I'll be right here by your side."

His words were one of the last things Fallon thought about as she drifted off to sleep, along with Gage's promise it wasn't over between them.

Pregnant.

Gage was still in shock over the news. He had absolutely no idea what to do with the information. He was equal parts overjoyed and scared out of his mind. He'd never thought about being a father because he'd never had one of his own. The closest he'd had to a father figure had been Henry Stewart and look how that had turned out.

But that didn't change the facts. Fallon was having his baby. He wasn't sure how far along she was, because they'd had a very active sex life, but he suspected she could have conceived as early as their honeymoon. During those idyllic days in Punta Cana he hadn't been able to get enough of her. He'd had a ferocious, all-consuming need for her. A need that had led them to creating a child.

But Fallon wanted nothing more to do with him. *Ever.*

She knew the truth that he'd been seeking to right the wrongs from years ago by acquiring stocks in Stewart Technologies. But she was wrong about his feelings for her. They'd grown exponentially and he was no longer seeking revenge. All he could see was Fallon. And now their baby.

Flashes of the two of them together holding a beautiful brown baby with hazel-gray eyes struck Gage. He walked to the bar and poured himself two thumbs of whiskey. Padding to the terrace, he lifted the glass to his mouth and sipped. The spirits warmed his insides but nothing could smooth out the raw edges from his reckoning with Fallon.

The disappointment in her eyes, the hurt—it dug into his insides. The thought he might never know his child, as he'd never known his father, was too much to deal with. He stared out at the city and sipped the whiskey as night fell over Austin. Somehow, some way, he had to change her mind. Make her realize her future and their baby's included him.

Seventeen

Muted voices slowly pulled Fallon back into consciousness. At first she didn't know where she was but then it dawned on her. She was in the hospital, fighting to keep her baby after nearly suffering a miscarriage.

Fallon blinked and opened her eyes. Her mother and father rushed to her side.

Her father spoke first. "You're awake. When we heard you'd fainted, your mother and I were scared to death. Thank you for calling us."

Henry turned and Fallon looked to see who he was speaking to. She noticed Ayden standing in the corner of the room, a haunted look on his face. Seconds later he walked out the door. It had taken courage for her big brother to make that call after their father had essentially abandoned him as a child. Fallon would be forever grateful. And she would tell Ayden that as soon as she had the chance.

"So, you're going to be a mommy," her mother stated with a wide grin. Nora came forward and lightly stroked her cheek. "You know, you're making me a grandma way before my time."

Fallon couldn't resist a smile.

"How far along are you?" her father asked. "If you don't mind my asking."

"Two months."

"You certainly didn't waste any time, my dear," her mother said. "It will certainly ensure Gage is on the hook for taking care of you and my grandson or grand-daughter for years to come."

Fallon sighed. Of course her mother thought in monetary terms. Fallon hoped Ayden hadn't told them Gage's true intentions and the reason she'd fainted. Her parents had no idea her marriage to Gage was over. Finished. She wouldn't stay married to someone who'd lied to and deceived her.

"Where's Gage?" Her father searched her eyes for an answer. "The mother of his child is in the hospital. Why isn't he here at your side?"

Fallon rubbed her temples. She was not in the mood for this. "Not now, Daddy."

"I agree, Henry," her mother said quietly. "Now isn't the time or place."

"Like hell it isn't. I smell a rat." Her father pressed on. "I had to hear about my daughter—" he pounded his chest "—from Ayden of all people. The son who hates me because I walked away from his mama. And you tell me I'm wrong?"

"What do you want from me, Daddy?" Fallon wailed. "For me to admit I made a mistake marrying Gage? Well, I did. There, I said it. Are you happy now?"

Her father's face clouded with unease and he came to sit by her bedside. "Of course I'm not happy to see my baby girl in pain. I only want what's best for you. That's all I have ever wanted."

Nervously, Fallon bit her lip and nodded as tears streamed down her cheeks. "Then let this go."

"All right." He nodded.

The nurse interrupted at the right moment when she came in with the cart to check Fallon's vitals.

"We're going to let you get some rest," her father said, giving her hand a gentle squeeze. "But we're a phone call away if you need us."

"Thank you, Daddy. And one other thing?"

"Anything, baby girl."

"It took a lot for Ayden to call you today, but he did it for me. Because he loves me. Please be kind to him."

"I will."

"Promise me."

"I promise."

After her parents departed and the nurse checked her blood pressure and pulse, Fallon glanced at her phone for messages. There was a text and a voice mail from Dane stating he was en route to Austin because Ayden had called him, too. Her big brother was pretty amazing. There were, however, no calls or texts from Gage. Had she been expecting one? She shouldn't.

She'd made it crystal clear she didn't want him near her, but theirs was only a cease-fire. Gage had *chosen* to leave, but he would be back. Of that she was sure.

The door to her room opened and Ayden returned. He'd long since abandoned the jacket and tie he'd come to her office in and was drinking what she suspected was coffee in a foam cup. He glanced around the room.

She read his mind. "They're gone."

He nodded and was quiet as he came to sit on the bed with her.

"Thank you for calling them. I really appreciate it. It must have been difficult dealing with our father after all this time. I know you didn't stay for the reception."

Ayden's hazel-gray eyes rested on her face. "You have no idea how hard, Fallon. When he arrived, there was no tearful reunion. He was here for you and you alone. It didn't matter that I was here, because I mean nothing to him."

Tears sprung to her eyes. "I'm sorry, Ayden."

He shrugged. "It's okay. I made my peace with it a long time ago. I'm glad I have you and Dane."

"So am I." Fallon attempted a half smile. "I owe you a great deal for looking out for me and bringing me your findings on Gage even though you knew it would hurt me."

"Honestly, Fallon, I struggled with whether I should tell you. I'd seen how happy you've been with Gage with my own eyes. Ultimately, after talking with Maya, she advised me I had to tell you, but it was hard. He clearly adores you and vice versa."

"That's a lie, Ayden." Tears brimmed in her eyes

and fell down her cheeks. "He was acting, giving me a false sense of security before he slipped the rug right out from under me. And as for me…" Her voice trailed off. "I foolishly thought somehow love would find a way. I thought in time my love might heal the pain and heartache he'd been through. I was wrong."

A wave of something close to desolation rushed through her. A sob broke free and she curled herself in the fetal position.

"It's okay, Fallon," Ayden whispered in her ear as he climbed onto the hospital bed and gathered her in his arms. "I'm here for you. Your big brother is here."

Days bled together in a dull gray jumble for Gage. He was trying not to mope and was focusing all his energy into work and managing his company's mutual funds. But it didn't lighten his mood. Instead he only grew bleaker as the days dragged on. Meanwhile he'd learned that Fallon had been released from the hospital with strict instructions to relax and avoid stress.

When he'd told Theo, his best friend had given him an I-told-you-so speech. Theo had advised Gage to grovel at Fallon's feet and beg her to take him back, but that was hard to do because, true to her word, she wanted nothing to do with him. She'd ignored every call or text he'd sent since her release. As for his mother, he couldn't tell her about the baby, not until he made things right with Fallon.

She'd sent Ayden and Maya to pack up her belongings at his penthouse. Gage had been sure not to be there; he hadn't wanted to see the sad looks on their faces.

His marriage was over when it should be thriving because they were having a child together. But he couldn't confront Fallon now and beat his chest about his rights. The doctor had told him she'd nearly miscarried and, in another month or so, she'd be out of the woods. Then they could tell everyone their great news.

And so Gage was giving Fallon the space she needed to get stronger so she could carry their child to term. She and the baby meant more to him than anything. He knew he didn't deserve either of them, but he would do his best by them. If she needed to relax in a stress-free zone and be with her family, then so be it.

He wasn't prepared, however, for her brother Dane to make an appearance at his office. The youngest Stewart was known to been MIA on most occasions. He hadn't even made their wedding, citing the excuse that he couldn't leave the movie he'd been filming, even though he was one of Hollywood's A-list actors.

"Dane." Gage rose when the six-foot-tall man approached him. He was what the ladies called a Pretty Ricky with café-au-lait skin, dark brown eyes and a perpetual five-o'clock shadow. He was wearing faded jeans, a graphic T-shirt, black boots and a leather jacket. Dane's good looks must have gotten him past Gage's assistant even though he'd given strict instructions to not be disturbed. "What can I do for you?"

"I came here to give you a black eye," Dane responded, making a fist and punching his other hand. "I heard about what you did to the company, but most of all to Fallon, how you played her for your own gain. And I came here to give you a piece of my mind."

"By all means," Gage responded, widening his arms. "Take your best shot. I deserve everything you have to say and then some."

Dane frowned. "You're not supposed to be helping this along."

"Why not? I know what I did was wrong. I apologized. Told Fallon I made a mistake and I should have never lied to her."

"Yet you did." Dane glared at him. "She feels like you made a fool of her. How could you do that? How can you stand to look at yourself in the mirror?" He crossed to Gage's desk and slammed his large hands on it. "Fallon has had a thing for you for years, Gage. And you knew that. You took advantage."

"I admit my intentions from the outset weren't honorable, but they changed when I fell in love with your sister."

"Love?" Dane laughed as he stood to his full six-foot height. "C'mon, Gage."

"It's true, Dane. I love Fallon and I love our baby."

Dane stared incredulously. "Does she know that?"

Gage shook his head. "That night…at the hospital. She never gave me a chance to say more. She ordered me out."

"Can you blame her?"

"No, I can't," Gage replied. "It's why I've stayed away, so she can calm down and get some rest. I don't want anything to happen to her or our baby."

Dane eyed him suspiciously. "You should know she

intends to divorce you. If you really love my sister, you don't have very long to fight for her."

"I know, but I will. You best believe that."

Fallon was ready to get back to work. Sitting on her bottom for the last two months had been sheer agony, but she would do anything to keep this baby safely in her womb. And she had. But she'd hated not being able to run her own company and be in the thick of the action.

Initially she'd been worried Gage would try to make a move on Stewart Technologies while she was out, but surprisingly it had been business as usual with no outside interference. It wouldn't last for long. One day soon Gage would make his move. In the meantime she enjoyed visits from her parents, Shana, Ayden and Maya. Even Dane had come during the early part of her convalescence to spend some time with her.

But she'd done as instructed and worked remotely from Stewart Manor to keep her stress level to a minimum. Initially she'd wanted to go back to her cottage, but her parents had been adamant that if something happened, they'd be too far away. They'd insisted she come home.

Nora fussed over her and was already knee-deep in discussion with an interior designer on decorating a nursery for when the baby came. Initially, Fallon was suspicious of Nora's motives. At the hospital her mother had made no secret of how her grandchild guaranteed Gage wouldn't be off the hook financially. But then Nora had surprised Fallon by offering to be her birth coach. It had been a rare mother-daughter moment, one that involved tears and hugs. But, of course, it was over much too quick. Nora wouldn't win mother of the year, but they were making inroads in their relationship. It seemed the baby was bringing them together.

Ayden and her father had gone from being civil to one another to actually having a conversation. They wouldn't be breaking into a hug anytime soon, but progress was being made. And if her personal suffering had caused a reunion between her big brother and father, then Fallon would gladly endure it.

Today, however, she was excited. After her checkup this morning at the four-month mark, she'd been given the green light to return to work next week. It felt like she'd been given a get-out-of-jail-free card.

She was leaving the doctor's office and heading to her car in the parking lot when she caught a familiar figure standing by her driver's-side door.

Gage.

She'd known it was possible he might show up. Although she didn't owe him a thing, she'd informed Gage of the doctor visit, but she'd urged him to stay away. When he hadn't shown, she'd thought she was in the clear. She'd been wrong.

Swallowing the lump in her throat, Fallon strolled toward him, hoping to give the appearance of nonchalance. Gage looked different. His eyes were haunted instead of intense as they usually were. He had on a leather jacket and faded jeans, which were hanging off him instead of clinging to his muscular thighs. *Had he lost weight?*

"How'd the doctor's visit go?"

"Fine."

"And the baby?"

"Is also fine," she replied. "We're both—"

"Fine, I know. I get that," Gage interrupted her. "Can we talk?"

"I believe your lawyers can handle whatever it is that requires discussion." Fallon used her key to unlock her door. "Can you step aside?"

Gage shook his head. "Fallon? We *have* to talk."

"Why? Because you say so?"

"Because we're having a baby. Do you honestly want other people deciding what's best for our child?"

Fallon sighed. "All right, there's a park across the street."

She began walking toward the crosswalk and noticed that Gage was still standing there. Had he been expecting her to hold his hand? He could think again. She watched him insert his hands into his pockets and move quickly to her side.

When they made it to the park, they sat on one of the many benches surrounding the playground. How apropos, considering one day they'd be watching a child of theirs running around and playing on the swings, slide and monkey bars.

Fallon turned to Gage. "Well, you wanted to talk. You have the floor."

Gage scooted around to face her. "Thank you for agreeing to talk to me."

"I doubt I had much choice."

"You have choices, Fallon," Gage responded, "and

I'm sorry if I made you feel like you didn't. I forced you into marrying me and didn't give you a whole lot of options."

"No, you didn't. I had forty-eight hours."

"I was afraid if I gave you too much time, you'd turn me down. And I had a plan to bring you and your family down a peg. It was all so easy when you're looking at it on paper, but after seeing you again, I was undone. I hadn't expected to be so completely enamored with you. I wanted you for myself."

"Do you honestly expect me to believe that?"

"I do. Look at how bullheaded I was. I wouldn't give you an inch. I requested we get married in a month's time."

Fallon sighed. "All right, so you lusted after me. That doesn't change the fact that you lied to me."

Gage stared her directly in the eye. "I did. And I can't take back what I've done. All I can do is tell you how incredibly sorry I am for hurting you. I never thought we'd have a real marriage, but somewhere along the line…" He paused. "Fallon, I fell in love you."

Her eyes widened in disbelief.

"I know you don't believe me," Gage said quickly. "Because I haven't earned your love. I used and abused your trust. I can only hope one day you'll believe me and let me be a father to our baby." He glanced down at her stomach, which was starting to show signs of rounding thanks to the child growing inside.

"Gage…"

"I love you, Fallon," he said again. "I probably always have and I certainly know I always will." He rose and lowered himself far enough to plant a kiss on her forehead. "And I believe what we had together was precious, but it wasn't built on the right foundation. One day it will be. I will prove to you I'm worthy of your love. I promise."

Stunned, Fallon watched Gage walk away. She sat on the bench until she heard school bells in the distance. Gage *loved* her. Why had it taken him so long to say the words she'd longed to hear? The words she'd felt so long for him but couldn't express for fear he didn't feel the same? Was he expressing his undying love for her because of the baby? He'd lied too easily and believably before. He'd made her think he wanted acceptance into society, all the while seducing her, when all he'd wanted was to ruin her family. No, as much as it pained her, she needed to listen to her gut. Gage didn't deserve her love or her trust.

Fallon patted her stomach and spoke to their baby. "I'm sorry we've made such a mess of this, but I'll fix it." Somehow, some way, she would. She would carve out a life for herself and this baby even if it didn't include its father.

"I have to admit your call was a surprise," Ayden said when Gage met up with him for drinks at a swanky downtown bar near both their offices a couple of weeks later.

"Even though I'm persona non grata in the Stewart family, I was hoping we could talk," Gage responded.

"If you're looking for help with Fallon," Ayden

began, "you can count me out. It's up to you to heal the wound in your relationship."

"Agreed. What'll you have?" He motioned to the bartender standing in front of Ayden.

"I'll have a whiskey." Ayden turned to Gage. "So, what's up? And has anyone told you that you look like hell?"

Gage smirked. He couldn't remember the last time he'd been to the barber for a haircut much less a trim to his beard. Nothing seemed to matter without Fallon in his life. He slid a large envelope toward Ayden.

Ayden's brow furrowed as he took it. "What's this?"

"Open it."

Ayden studied him for a long moment before sliding his finger under the flap and opening the envelope. He pulled out a stack of papers and read through them. Then those hazel-gray eyes so like Fallon's stared at him in shock. "Why would you do this?"

"To prove to Fallon I only want her and our baby."

"But why me?" Ayden inquired. When the waiter returned with his drink, he took a long swallow.

"Because they're rightfully yours. They belong to you," Gage responded. "Call it righting a wrong done to you and your mother. I know Henry cheated your mother out of her shares. I'm only giving you what you deserve."

"I can't let you do this, Gage," Ayden responded. "This is a fortune. I'm sure there's another way to prove yourself to Fallon. Plus, I'm not even sure how I feel about this. I mean, I'm not a part of the Stewart family."

"My spies tell me otherwise. I heard you've been visiting Stewart Manor."

"To see Fallon." Ayden's voice rose slightly. "Although Henry and I are polite to one another for Fallon's sake, we're far from bosom buddies. And even if I were to accept your generous offer, how would this look to Fallon? She might think you and I were in it together all along to get revenge against Henry because we both have a beef with him. I don't want to ruin the relationship we have. Fallon and I have grown close."

Gage slid off the bar stool and threw back the last bit of whiskey he'd been drinking. "You and I know the truth. We were never in cahoots to cheat Fallon. Just me. I'm the scoundrel and she knows that. You have to trust in what you've built with her. As for the others, do you really care what Henry thinks?"

Ayden gave him a sidelong glance. "Once upon a time I did, but not anymore."

"Well then, you're a Stewart, Ayden. Take what's yours. Take what should have been your inheritance. I have no right to it and neither does Fallon. I hope she'll understand the reasoning behind my decision."

"I hope to God you're right," Ayden said, grabbing the papers and scribbling his name on them. "And I don't regret this decision. But, yes, on my mother's behalf for everything she was denied from Henry, I accept."

Leaving the bar, Gage had never felt so good. The last two months he'd been tormented by his actions. Each morning he woke up feeling as if something had broken inside him. It had. But tonight he'd relieved himself of the one thing standing between him and a second chance with his wife. He hoped it was enough to prove he loved and wanted Fallon and their baby.

Fallon still couldn't believe what Ayden had shared with her. Gage had given Ayden all of the stock he'd acquired in Stewart Technologies. And he hadn't sold it to him. He'd *given* them to her big brother lock, stock and barrel, without asking for anything in return.

It was a generous gesture and Ayden explained that at first he wasn't entirely sure what to do. But then he told her why he'd said yes. His mother, Lillian, had helped his father start Stewart Technologies, but during the divorce she'd been outgunned by Henry's fancy lawyers and had walked away with a small settlement. Ayden felt it was okay to accept Gage's gift. And Fallon had agreed. He'd been surprised Fallon wasn't angry with Gage for not offering them to her first.

She wasn't. Yet Ayden had offered to share the stock Gage had given *him* with her. He wanted to prove he wasn't in cahoots with Gage on a takeover, but Fallon turned Ayden down and told him to keep the stock. She already ran Stewart Technologies and had shares in the company herself. She didn't need more. But Ayden? He'd been abandoned by their father. Fallon was ashamed Henry acted as if Ayden didn't exist. He'd never even paid child support, much less acknowledged Ayden's accomplishments. The shares were his just deserts. She was surprised Gage had understood that and hadn't wanted to keep them for himself. After everything that had happened to Gage and his mother, she was certain he felt entitled to them, but he hadn't. Instead he'd offered them to Ayden.

A man who, like Gage, had been looked down on.

She doubted her father would agree with her. He would be livid that Ayden, the black sheep, had leverage over him. But Fallon didn't mind if Ayden had a larger stake in Stewart Technologies than she did. She was CEO and running the company, after all. Ayden had his own company, Stewart Investments, to worry about.

What she couldn't get over was Gage's generous act. It gave her hope that there was some humanity left in him. That he was a man she could love. A man who could be a father to her baby.

And so today she'd decided to hop in her Audi and drive to see her bullheaded, arrogant and controlling husband to find out if she was still living in a fairy-tale world where love won out in the end.

She didn't waste time parking when she arrived at Gage's building; she merely tossed her keys to the valet, waved at the doorman and rushed to the private elevator. She pressed the code for the penthouse and impatiently waited for the car to ascend to the top. She paced the travertine-tiled floor until finally the doors opened into the penthouse.

The apartment was dark and Fallon wondered if Gage was home, but then she saw a figure in silhouette outside on the terrace. It was Gage's favorite place to go when he needed to think things over. The pocket doors were open so the click of her heels as she approached caused Gage to turn around in his chair. Her heart quickened at the sight of him.

"Fallon?" His voice was raspy.

When she was within a few feet of him, she answered. "Yes, it's me." She noticed the glass in his hand with a dark liquid she could only assume was brandy, his drink of choice.

"I thought perhaps I was dreaming like I have been the last couple of months, hoping you'd come home. That you'd come back to me. Is that why you're here? Are you back for good?"

Fallon stared at him from where she stood. He looked haggard, with lines around his eyes, and his beard had grown. When was the last time he'd shaved? "I don't know, Gage, that depends on how this conversation goes."

The hope she'd given him instantly caused him to straighten and he walked toward her until they were face-to-face.

"Why did you do it, Gage?" Fallon asked, searching his face. "Why did you give Ayden those shares?"

"Because they're rightfully his," Gage responded. "Always should have been. I had no right to them. I was angry and acquired them as a way to get back at your father. To strike him where it hurts. Then he would see I was good enough for you. But you know what?"

"What?"

"The person I hurt most was you. The woman I've come to love. And as a result, I hurt myself because you left me. Alone. How I've always been."

She dragged in a sustaining breath. "Gage…" Her

heart broke for him even though he was the reason they were in this situation to begin with.

"I know I have no right to ask you this." His eyes pierced hers as he held her gaze. "Can you forgive me for being such a stupid, arrogant, bullish fool in search of power and prestige? I can't change the man I was, but because of you I can change and be the man you need me to be—a whole, mature man." He glanced around and his mouth twisted in pain. "Because none of it means anything without you, Fallon. I'm sorry. Your being here gives me hope that perhaps—perhaps—you might be willing to give us another chance. A chance to be a family. Because I want more than anything to be married to you."

Fallon didn't move. She stayed where she was. Her heart galloped in her chest. She was afraid to move, let alone speak, because her heart was so full. She felt the tears silently slide down her cheeks one by one. She felt the moisture against her skin but was suspended in time with Gage as she always was whenever he was near.

"Please don't shut me out of your life, Fallon. Please let me be near you and our baby." Gage reached out and cupped her cheek. "Don't cry, please. That's not what I want." Slowly he pulled her to him, cradling her in his arms.

It was her undoing. His words were scraping away all her defenses, all the walls she'd erected around herself. Fallon knew why Gage had been so generous and why he'd given those shares to Ayden. He wanted to prove that he wanted her more than his quest for revenge. The truth blazed in her heart, sure and true. Gage was the man she loved. The man she'd always loved. Whom she would love forever.

"I love you." The words escaped her lips before she had a chance to take them back. And as she said them, the heaviness she'd felt for weeks began to lighten.

It was an indelible fact. She could never stop loving Gage. He'd had her from the moment he'd helped her after she'd fallen off that horse. "Totally. Uncontrollably. And with all my heart."

"Oh, God, Fallon, I love you, too, so much." His voice sounded choked.

They reached for each other at the same time. Their eyes locked in a hot, heated moment before he bowed his head and he brushed his lips across hers. The slow, sweet kiss caused a low moan to release from her lips. Oh, how she'd missed this. And when he angled his head so he could deepen the kiss and take full possession of her mouth, Fallon was on board. She slid her tongue against his and the taste of him exploded in her mouth.

A slow curl of heat unraveled in her as she tangled her arms around his neck. It had been too long—far too long—since he'd touched her like this. Kissed her like this.

"Gage," she murmured when they came up for air. She took in large gulps, breathing in his dark, delicious scent that was so real and achingly familiar. Peace filled her as Gage held her to his hard, solid chest. "Make love to me," she whispered.

"With pleasure." In seconds he'd swept her into his arms and carried her down the hall to their bed.

Gage laid his beautiful wife down on *their* bed and smiled as she hurriedly removed her clothing and his until he could lie beside her. Catching a whiff of her delicate floral scent awakened every cell in his body and revived memories of how good it had been between them. It had been those images that had haunted him in the weeks they'd been apart, tormenting his mind and his body. He'd been unable to sleep and it showed in the tiredness he'd felt each day.

Until now. He considered himself lucky Fallon was forgiving him. He would have another chance to be a better husband and a father to their child.

He looked down at her in bewilderment. "Is it really possible we can try again? Start afresh?"

Fallon reached for him then, wrapping her arms around his neck and bestowing him with sweet, tender kisses. And Gage realized what true forgiveness looked like.

"Good. Because I want to give you everything," Gage said.

Their lovemaking that night was slow and worshipful because there was nothing but love and joy between them. They found their way back to each other's bodies, exploring every available inch while whispering loving words that would blanket them and last them a lifetime. Until, eventually, sleep claimed them as they lay in each other's arms.

Epilogue

A year later

Fallon emerged from the bedroom where she'd gone to change clothes—for the second time that day—after her son, Dylan, had chosen to throw up all over her baptism outfit. But she didn't care. Fallon felt as if she were the luckiest woman in the world.

She and Gage were as in love as ever. She never knew she could be this happy. This fulfilled. Months ago they'd renewed their vows. It had been just the two of them and they'd pledged to start over. And they had. They were rebuilding Stewart Technologies with some help from her big brother. Ayden had chosen to keep the stock and hoped to give it to his children someday. Her parents, her father especially, had initially blustered over Gage's gift, but eventually he'd piped down when he'd realized pitting Fallon against her big brother could cause him to lose her.

Fallon and Gage had been thrilled. And when they'd attended Ayden and Maya's wedding on Valentine's Day, it had brought tears to Fallon's eyes. Gage had incorrectly thought she was upset over their first ceremony, but then she'd told him, she'd been in love with him even then and they'd kissed and made out like two love-struck teenagers in the back of the reception hall.

Fallon smiled at the memory as she walked down the corridor of their new house, which wasn't far from Stewart Manor so her parents could be close to their grandson. Before Dylan's arrival, she and Gage had decided they'd need more space, a house that was kid-friendly instead of Gage's ultra-chic penthouse. He kept it as an investment and for the nights he worked late in the city, but those days were over for Fallon. Once she'd had Dylan, she'd cut back on her hours. She wanted to be a better mother than Nora had been.

When she arrived at the terrace where they were hosting the reception after the baptism, Fallon glanced at her mother, who was in a battle with Grace for the title of most doting grandmother. Both women had called a cease-fire when Fallon told them in no uncertain terms she would cut them off from seeing the baby if they didn't behave. Nora and Grace would never be friends, but they'd learned to coexist. It surprised Fallon to see another side to Nora—a kind, caring, compassionate side she'd never had, but of which she was glad Dylan would be the beneficiary.

However, right now, he was getting a little fussy and was starting to cry.

"I'll take him." Fallon reached for her son.

"Are you sure?" Grace asked. "Because I don't mind holding him."

"Yeah, I'm properly prepared now," Fallon stated, having procured a burping cloth to lay over her shoulder. She accepted her son from his grandmother.

"He's so beautiful." Nora stroked her grandson's curly black hair while Fallon held him and patted his bottom, soothing his loud cries.

"What'd you expect?" her father interjected from nearby where he was huddled with her husband, Dane, Ayden and Maya. It wasn't hearts and roses between the men she loved, but they were all trying to be cordial for her sake and for Dylan's. "He's a Stewart."

"And a Campbell," Gage said as he made his way over to Fallon.

She glanced up at her husband and love shone so clearly in his eyes. She couldn't believe how lucky she was they'd found each other again. It hadn't been an easy road getting here, but they'd made it through the storm.

Gage bowed his head and brushed a tender kiss across her lips. "Have I told you how much I love you?"

Fallon grinned and paused a moment. "No—" she shook her head "—I don't believe you have today."

"Well, then, let me remedy that. I love you, Fallon Stewart Campbell, and you're the only woman for me."

"And you, Gage Campbell, are all the man I need."

* * * * *

You won't want to miss Dane's story,
coming soon from Yahrah St. John
and Harlequin Desire.

COMING NEXT MONTH FROM

Available September 3, 2019

#2683 TEXAS-SIZED SCANDAL
Texas Cattleman's Club: Houston • by Katherine Garbera
Houston philanthropist Melinda Perry always played by the rules. Getting pregnant by a mob boss's son was certainly never in the playbook—until now. Can they contain the fallout...and maybe even turn their forbidden affair into forever?

#2684 STRANDED AND SEDUCED
Boone Brothers of Texas • by Charlene Sands
To keep her distance from ex-fling Risk Boone, April Adams pretends to be engaged. But when a storm strands them together and the rich rancher has an accident resulting in amnesia, he suddenly thinks he's the fiancé! Especially when passion overtakes them...

#2685 BLACK TIE BILLIONAIRE
Blackout Billionaires • by Naima Simone
CEO Gideon Knight demands that Shay Neal be his fake fiancée to avenge his family. Too bad he doesn't realize they already shared an anonymous night during the Chicago blackout! But even through the deception, the truth of their chemistry cannot be denied.

#2686 CALIFORNIA SECRETS
Two Brothers • by Jules Bennett
Ethan Michaels is on a mission to reclaim the resort his mother built. Then he's sidetracked by sexy Harper Williams—only to find out she's his enemy's daughter. All's fair in love and war...until Harper's next explosive secret shakes Ethan to his core.

#2687 A BET WITH BENEFITS
The Eden Empire • by Karen Booth
Entrepreneur Mindy Eden scoffs when her sisters bet she can't spend time with her real estate mogul ex without succumbing to temptation. But it soon becomes crystal clear that second chances are in the cards. Will Mindy risk her business for one more shot at pleasure?

#2688 POWER PLAY
The Serenghetti Brothers • by Anna DePalo
Hockey legend and sports industry tycoon Jordan Serenghetti needs his injury healed—and fast. Too bad he clashes with his physical therapist over a kiss they once shared—and Jordan forgot! As passions flare, will she be ready for more revelations from his player past?

**YOU CAN FIND MORE INFORMATION ON UPCOMING HARLEQUIN® TITLES,
FREE EXCERPTS AND MORE AT WWW.HARLEQUIN.COM.**

HDCNM0819

SPECIAL EXCERPT FROM

HQN™

For Vanessa Logan, returning home was about healing, not exploring her attraction to cowboy Jacob Dalton! But walking away from their explosive chemistry is proving impossible…

Read on for a sneak preview of
Lone Wolf Cowboy *by* New York Times *and*
USA TODAY *bestselling author Maisey Yates.*

She curled her hands into fists, grabbing hold of his T-shirt. And she had no idea what the hell was running through her head as she stood there looking up into those wildly blue eyes, the present moment mingling with memories of that night long ago.

While he witnessed the deepest, darkest thing she'd ever gone through. Something no one else even knew about.

He was the only one who knew.

The only one who knew what had started everything. Olivia didn't understand. Her parents didn't understand. And they had never wanted to understand.

But he knew. He knew and he had already seen what a disaster she was.

There was no facade to protect. No new enlightened sense of who she was. No narrative about her as a lost cause out there roaming the world.

He'd already seen her break apart. For real. Not the Vanessa that existed when she was hiding. Hiding her problems from her family. Hiding her feelings behind a high.

Hiding. And more hiding.

No. He had seen her at her lowest when she hadn't been able to hide.

And somehow, he seemed to bring that out in her. Because she wasn't able to hide her anger.

And she wasn't able to hide this. Whatever the wildness was that was coursing through her veins. No, she couldn't hide that either. And she wasn't sure she cared.

So she was just going to let the wildness carry her forward.

She couldn't remember the last time she had done that. The last time she'd allowed herself this pure kind of over-the-top emotion.

It had been pain. The pain she felt that night she lost the baby. That was the last time she had let it all go. In all the time since then when she had been on the verge of being overwhelmed by emotion she had crushed it completely. Hidden it beneath drugs. Hidden it beneath therapy speak.

She had carefully kept herself in hand since she'd gotten sober. Kept herself under control.

What she hadn't allowed herself to do was feel.

She was feeling now. And she wasn't going to stop it.

She launched herself forward, and her lips connected with his.

And before she knew it, she was kissing Jacob Dalton with all the passion she hadn't known existed inside of her.

Don't miss
Lone Wolf Cowboy *by Maisey Yates,*
available August 2019 wherever
Harlequin® books and ebooks are sold.

www.Harlequin.com

"To answer your other question," he murmured. "Why did I
single you out? Your first guess was correct. Because you are
so beautiful I couldn't help following you around this over-
the-top ballroom filled with people who possess more money
than sense. The women here can't outshine you. They're like
peacocks, spreading their plumage, desperate to be noticed,
and here you are among them, like the moon. Bright, alone,
above it all and eclipsing every one of them. What I don't
understand is how no one else noticed before me. Why every
man in this place isn't standing behind me in a line just for
the chance to be near you."

Silence swelled around them like a bubble, muting the din
of the gala. His words seemed to echo in the cocoon, and he
marveled at them. Hadn't he sworn he didn't do pretty words?
Yet it had been him talking about peacocks and moons.

What was she doing to him?

Even as the question echoed in his mind, her head tilted
back and she stared at him, her lovely eyes darker…hotter. In

that moment, he'd stand under a damn balcony and serenade her if she continued looking at him like that. He curled his fingers into his palm, reminding himself with the pain that he couldn't touch her. Still, the only sound that reached his ears was the quick, soft pants breaking on her pretty lips.

"I—I need to go," she whispered, already shifting back and away from him. "I—" She didn't finish the thought, but turned and waded into the crowd, distancing herself from him.

He didn't follow; she hadn't said no, but she hadn't said yes, either. And though he'd caught the desire in her gaze—his stomach still ached from the gut punch of it—she had to come to him.

Or ask him to come for her.

Rooted where she'd left him, he tracked her movements.

Saw the moment she cleared the mass of people and strode in the direction of the double doors where more tray-bearing staff emerged and exited.

Saw when she paused, palm pressed to one of the panels.

Saw when she glanced over her shoulder in his direction.

Even across the distance of the ballroom, the electric shock of that look whipped through him, sizzled in his veins. Moments later, she disappeared from view. Didn't matter; his feet were already moving in her direction.

That glance, that look. It'd sealed her fate.

Sealed it for both of them.

What will happen when these two find each other alone during the blackout?

Find out in
Black Tie Billionaire
by USA TODAY *bestselling author Naima Simone available September 2019 wherever Harlequin® Desire books and ebooks are sold.*

www.Harlequin.com

HDEXP0819